OSCAR
THE DETECTIVE

MORE WILDSIDE CLASSICS

Please see www.wildsidepress.com for a complete list!

OSCAR THE DETECTIVE

OR, DUDIE DUNNE, THE EXQUISITE DETECTIVE.

An Odd but Stirring Detective Narrative.

BY OLD SLEUTH

WILDSIDE PRESS

OSCAR THE DETECTIVE

This edition published in 2006 by Wildside Press, LLC.
www.wildsidepress.com

CHAPTER I

DUDIE DUNNE PLAYS A GREAT TRICK TO RUN
DOWN A CRIMINAL — AS SIMPLE JOHN HE
APPEARS INNOCENT, BUT WHEN HIS MASK GOES
OFF THE "FUR FLIES."

"Oh, fellers, look at this! he's strayed or stolen; let's go for him."

A group of little toughs were gathered at a street corner in a low locality in the city of New York when a dude of the first water with the regular Anglo step and exquisite airs walked leisurely down the street peering through his single eyeglass at the surrounding tenements. He was a splendid specimen in appearance of the dudie sweet, and the moment the eyes of the gamins fell upon him they saw a chance for fun. It was at first intended as a raid for fun, but in the end it became plunder.

The dude walked along until he arrived opposite the spot where the boys were gathered, where they lay like little Indians in ambush ready to leap forth to slaughter. The dude stopped short, gazed at them with a smile which was all simplicity and asked:

"Can you boys tell me where Maggie's aunt lives around here? Tell me and I'll give you a cent apiece."

"Here!" said one of the boys, and a second queried:

"What is it?"

"Where did this thing drop from?"

"Well, ain't he a sweetie!"

"Oh, dear boys, I am so weary. I've been looking for Maggie's aunt. She lives somewhere down here. Maggie is our cook and she is under the weather — yes, very much under the weather — and I agreed to notify her aunt, but hang me if I can find her aunt. I don't know her aunt's name; I forgot to ask her what her dear aunt's name is, and all I know is that she lives down this way somewhere, and she is Maggie's aunt. If you lads will take me to her I will give you a penny apiece — I will, yes — I am in earnest — hee, hee, hee!"

The laugh was something to hear, and the lads, all in chorus, imitated the simpleton's laugh with a "hee, hee, hee!" which sounded very ridiculous, and the dude said:

"Oh, you rude boys, I really believe you are mocking me — yes, I do. Now don't be naughty, but come and show me where Maggie's aunt lives — hee, hee, hee!"

Again the lads in chorus "hee, hee, hee-d."

"Boys, what have we struck?" came the question.

"Now don't be rude, boys, don't be rude, or I will chastise you — yes, I will chastise you. I don't want to do so, but you may compel me to chastise you."

The boys just roared at this threat, and one of them stealing behind the dude gave him a "thumper" with his toe where the exquisite's pants were drawn the tightest under his long coat.

"Oh, oh, you wicked boy! What do you mean? Stop, I say, stop, or I'll call the police, yes, I will."

"Say, Dudie, there are no police around here; we slaughtered and burned 'em all last month; you'll find their graves down under the rocks there, so don't holler."

As the spokesman uttered the words quoted he let drive and knocked off the dude's hat, which one of the gang immediately appropriated, and then the onslaught commenced. They just tore at the poor dude as a wolf tears at a carcass, and in less time than it takes to tell it they had stripped the poor fellow. One had put on the long coat and commenced to walk English style, another donned the robbed man's hat, a second secured the eyeglass, a third his undercoat, a fourth his nobby vest, and so they stripped him of all his outside apparel, assumed it themselves, and then the circus commenced. They just paraded around their poor victim, imitating in a grotesque manner all the airs of a genuine dudie sweet. Two or three rough-looking men were standing at the door of a low groggery opposite and they enjoyed the fun and laughed as merrily as the boys who were conducting the affair. "What have we struck?" the lads kept repeating, and the dude stood denuded to his shirt and trousers, appealing to the lads to restore his wardrobe, and his appeals were pitiable to hear.

"Oh, boys, you good boys, now you've had lots of fun, but dear me, I'll freeze — yes, it's an awful good joke — hee, hee, hee — but I'll freeze, and to think, boys, how I look! Why, I'll become a laughing-stock, but it's an awful good joke — yes, I've enjoyed it; we've had lots of fun — hee, hee, hee — but now restore my clothing, please do."

The boys instead of returning the dude's clothes began to maltreat him. They kicked and cuffed him around until one of the men walked over and said:

"Here, you rascals, stop this now."

Another of the men came, and they seized the lads one after the other, took the stolen clothes away from them and restored the goods to their rightful owner. Well, this may appear very nice on the part of the men, but the sequel will show that they were actuated entirely by selfish motives. They discerned that the dude might prove good plucking for themselves, and they were very kind and consoling as they assisted him to resume his garments and he said:

"Well, we've had lots of fun, the poor dear boys; I did feel as though they went too far and I should punish them, but I hadn't the heart — no, I haven't the heart — I am so tender-hearted. I am almost a woman when it comes to the heart, everybody says so."

The men exchanged winks and laughed. It looked to them as very ridiculous — this delicate-looking dude punishing that gang of rough and vigorous gamins.

The dude was speedily re-robed and one of the men said:

"Let's go over and have a drink."

"Thank you, gentlemen, thank you, I am much obliged certainly. We shall have a drink, but I will treat — yes, I will treat. But didn't we have fun! and I am so glad I maintained my temper and did not hurt those poor little boys. It was all play, you know — gentlemen, all play. I enjoyed it very much — yes, very much."

"They were getting a little rough," said one of the men.

"Yes, but you know I was getting a little rough myself. Really, I hope I didn't hurt any of them. I didn't mean to. I'm very vigorous, for I belong to an athletic club. I dare not trust myself to play rough with men, let alone boys — yes, I didn't dare strike. I didn't want to hurt any of them."

"You were very gentle," said one of the men.

"I intended to be. Yes, I am as gentle as a lamb unless I am aroused, then I become a lion — everybody says so — yes, I am very ferocious when I get mad, and I have to restrain myself."

"I can see you are very powerful. I wouldn't like to provoke you," said the man with a wink to his companions and an unrestrained look of contempt.

"I hope you never may. No, I do not like to lose my temper. I become very rough — yes, very rough indeed, my friends all tell me so; but I like fun — yes, I am a thoroughbred, I am, clean through. I gamble, I do — yes, I am a regular sport, and I am so glad I did not hurt any of those boys."

"Yes, you were very considerate."

"Oh, certainly, I am always considerate — my friends all say so. I am naturally kind and gentle, but terrible when I get aroused — yes, I am just awful; so, gentlemen, don't provoke me in any way."

"You can bet we won't provoke you. I tell you I don't want to get it in the eye from one of those mauleys of yours, and get knocked into the middle of next week."

"Hee, hee, hee! how observant you are, and now you've really discovered that I am an athlete! Well, I try not to betray the fact — yes, I am very careful to not let people know, and I try to keep my temper. I don't like to get aroused."

The men went into the barroom and the dude called for a bottle of wine, and the miserable apology for wine was put on the counter. As the dude pulled forth a big wad of bills to pay for it the eyes of the men glittered and they exchanged winks and looked longingly at the roll of greenbacks.

The wine was consumed and the dude ordered cigars, and he became quite talkative and drank a glass of whisky that was placed before him. Then he became still more talkative, and all the time he was the dude to perfection and boasted of his powers.

"Do you know," he said, "I once had a run in with —?"

The man named was a noted boxer.

"How did you come out with him?"

"Oh, I was gentle with him — very gentle. He winked and I understood what he meant and let up on him and permitted him to punch me. Yes, it was business with him, you know, and I could have knocked him out before all his pupils, so I just let him punch me."

"He is a pretty hard hitter they say."

"Oh, no, I didn't mind his blows. He is very active — yes, very active."

"Did he bleed you?"

"Oh, yes, I let him bleed me a little. I was gentle, you know, and I took a black eye which I carried for a week, and he afterward apologized. Yes, he was very grateful because I was so gentle and let him punch me. I spared him, but when I looked in the glass I told him that next time I'd have to rap back a little."

The men all laughed and one of them said: "I reckon he will not tackle you again?"

"No, I guess not — hee, hee, hee! I tell you when I threaten a man he looks out — yes, he does — hee, hee, hee!"

"I reckon you are a lucky gambler."

"You bet I am."

"Yes, you educated fellows are always quick in making combinations. I like to play with a good player and learn his 'points.' I am always ready to lose to learn. What do you say for a little game with a light ante?"

"Well, now see here, I don't want to rob you gentlemen — you've been so kind to me."

"Oh, we don't mind losing a few dollars. You see, we are contractors. We do big jobs for the city; we've plenty of money, only we ain't educated, see, that's all. We've worked our way in the world. We are self-made men."

"Well, do you know, I've got the highest regard for self-made men. My daddy was a self-made man. He was a government contractor, and when he died he left my mamma a million, and it will all come to me some day. Yes, I am the lucky only child, I am; but I don't want to rob you gentlemen."

"Oh, we've all plenty of money to lose, and it's an honor to play with a real gentleman. We don't always have that privilege, and it's real condescending in you."

"Oh, yes, I am very condescending — yes, yes — hee, hee, hee! But really I'd only rob you gentlemen. I call you gentlemen because you are gentlemen. I always judge of a man as I find him, as Bobby Burns bid us do, see — hee, hee, hee!"

The party had drank several times and the dude began to show the effect of his drinks. He was a dude as true and genuine as ever lived.

"Let's go upstairs and have a quiet game," said the man; "we don't want to play down here where we will be disturbed by every low fellow that comes in. I tell you, gentlemen, we must protect our guest from annoyance — he is so kind as to give us a game and teach us a few points."

"Say, gentlemen, I am not aristocratic; I don't put on airs; I'd just as soon play down here."

"No, it is much nicer upstairs. We can have a quiet game and take our refreshments," and addressing the bartender the man asked:

"Are you putting up the best every time, Sandy?"

"Sure, I do; I knows me business, I do; I knows when a gentleman stands in front of the bar."

Young reader, this may be a lonely sort of siren play,

but it is true to life and should prove a lesson. The men were flattering the dude, and flattery is always based on design and a selfish motive. Beware of the flatterer in the first place. Eschew gambling — if you are only playing for fun it costs as much as though you were playing to make money. It is demoralizing every time, and often leads to greater crime. Gambling is a very dangerous amusement. These men were working the dude, and it is, as we have intimated, an actual incident we are describing. The conversation we reproduce verbatim. They were alluring the young man to rob him, and if the stake had been big enough these birds of prey would willingly have murdered their victim in the end to cover up the lesser crime with the greater, for they were believers in the false logic that "dead men tell no tales." We say false logic, for dead men, though their lips are silent, as a rule — ay, almost always — leave silent testimonies behind that speak for them, and crime is always revealed. The silence of the murdered is a dangerous release, for murder "will out," though, as stated, the lips of the victims are sealed in death.

Dudie Dunne played well his part. He did not readily consent to go upstairs. He was playing a great game, playing on novel plans, taking great chances, and for the rascals who were alluring him he had a great surprise in reserve.

After much persuasion he consented to go upstairs, but still continued to assure the men that he had no idea of robbing them.

"But you will teach us some new points."

"You'll have to watch me then, for I am giving nothing away."

The men ascended to a room on the second floor, a rear room.

The men sat down at a table and Dudie Dunne put on all the airs of a "Smart Alec" to perfection. The game commenced. Our hero was dealer and a winner, and the way he "hee, hee, hee-d," as he raked in his pot was amusing to watch.

The game proceeded for fully half an hour when a most startling interruption occurred.

CHAPTER II

THE EXQUISITE'S GAME PROVES A WINNING HAND, BUT NOT AT THE CARDS — HE PERFORMS ONE OF THE GREATEST STREAKS OF DETECTIVE WORK TO DATE AND CAPTURES A MAN WHOM FIVE THOUSAND DOLLARS REWARD HAD FAILED TO FETCH.

As intimated, the game had proceeded and our hero was winning and losing, when suddenly the door of the room opened and a man of remarkable appearance entered the room. His entrance was followed by an exhibition as though a ghost had suddenly appeared at the conventional midnight hour and demanded a hand, as he reached forth his rattling joints of bone. The men stared, even our hero for just one instant lost his equipoise, but he recovered when like a wink he asked, as though no one had entered the room:

"What do you do?"

The men, however, just sat and stared while the intruder said, a pallor on his emaciated face and a glitter in his eyes:

"I heard the game going on, boys, and I could not resist — oh, I love a little game at times."

"You are not well enough to sit up yet, Mr. Alling."

"Oh, yes; I feel better to-day; but whom have we here?"

One of the men winked and said:

"A friend of ours — one of the four hundred — but he ain't proud. He is a gentleman clean through."

The man who had asked the question fixed his glittering eyes on our hero. The dude appeared unconscious of the fact that he was undergoing a study beneath the gaze of a man who could read the human face like a book.

As intimated, the man was a very remarkable-looking individual. He was one who would attract attention anywhere, owing to the singular sharp expression on his face.

The man appeared to be satisfied with his study, and said, as he sat down to the table: "Give me some cards. Ah, this is just glorious after having lain in a sick bed for a month."

The dude, who was studying his cards, did not appear to overhear the newcomer's remark. He had been a loser and seemed absolutely absorbed.

The game proceeded and drinks were ordered. The dude got seemingly very drunk. He lost his money — some hundreds of dollars, and his watch, and produced a diamond pin which he lost, and then he appeared to drop off in a maudlin slumber.

The man let him snore in his chair and deliberately divided his money among them. Then they dealt for the watch and pin, and finally the question was asked:

"What shall we do with him?"

"Throw him into the street."

"That won't do," said the man who had entered the room at the last moment. "You fellows don't know how to manage these things."

"What shall we do?"

"Let him sleep. He will sleep until morning — sleep like a top — and then the first thing he will call for will be a drink; give him one, then take him to some other house, fill him up, and leave him one by one. He will forget afterward where he lost his watch and money. At least you fellows can all swear he had his watch and money when you left him. Throw him into the street, and he will be found, dragged in, and in the morning will give the whole business away. That is the way you lads always make a mistake. You don't go slow enough."

The men agreed to Alling's plan, and then turning the dude over on the floor, fixed his coat under his head for a pillow and left him, locking him in the room, and there the poor dude lay. One of the men returned in about half an hour, looked the sleeper over and left. Downstairs he told his pals:

"He will never wake. I reckon the man is full to the ears. He will sleep until eleven o'clock to-morrow."

After the man had glanced into the room the dude most strangely awoke. He drew from his pocket a tiny mask lantern, and he pulled a tiny watch from his pocket, glanced at the time and muttered:

"I've got a long wait, but it's all right. I'll have my man."

The hours passed. The dude lay upon the floor and actually slept a natural sleep, but after some hours he awoke, glanced at his watch and muttered:

"Now it is time to operate."

He rose from his coat pillow and put his coat on, fixed himself to go to the street, then deftly opened the door of the room, peeped out and listened. All was still. Indeed it was two o'clock in the morning. The dude passed down the stairs, and through the hall to the street door. He unlocked it as deftly as he had unlocked the room door. He put it just in the swing, then he ascended the stairs and passed to the top floor of the house. He knew just where to go for the purpose he had in hand, for he had overheard a little while he was being robbed at the game of cards. He stopped at the rear room door and listened, then he deftly opened the door and drew from his pocket the tiny mask lantern. He flashed the slenderest of lines of light toward the bed and thereon lay a man. Could one have pierced the darkness at that moment and have seen the face of the dude it would have been a most startling revelation, especially to one who had seen him some hours previously.

The dude on tiptoe advanced toward the bed. Quickly he clapped a silken handkerchief to the mouth and nostrils of the sleeping man, and then from the big dude coat he drew a gag and some cords; quickly he proceeded and soon had the man gagged and bound. A moment only he rested, and then the dude, the delicate-looking dude, after having slipped on a few outside garments, raised the bound and gagged man in his arms, handled him as though he had been an unresisting lad of ten or twelve years, and carried him down two pair of stairs to the street door. He stepped forth and walked off with his burden. He met no one until he had traversed several squares, when a policeman accosted him:

"Hold on! what have you there — a dead body?"

"No, a man pretty thoroughly alive, and I want your aid — he is getting heavy."

The dude made an explanation and the policeman aided in carrying the man. He was taken to the station house, where the gag was removed, also the cords, and the man was free.

"Who is he, Dunne?" asked the sergeant in charge.

The dude whispered a name and the sergeant started back aghast.

"How did you pick him up?"

"Oh, it's a long tale, but I've got him."

Handcuffs were put on the prisoner and, accompanied by two detectives, Detective Dunne started with his man for headquarters. The fellow Alling meantime said, speaking to the supposed dude:

"You played it well, but your play will cost your life in the end."

"Hush, Jimmy, don't threaten while the darbies are on you; but it will be a long time before you will again enjoy your favorite game."

"One word, Dunne."

"Go it."

"Was I betrayed?"

"No."

"Those fellows didn't give you the pointers to get a whack at the reward offered on me?"

"No."

"That is square between a square man and a thief?"

"It is the truth."

"You swear it?"

"I do."

"All right, I am to hold you alone responsible for this?"

"Yes."

"You worked it out yourself?"

"I did. Your pals don't know yet you are gone."

"Oh, I wish I had suspected."

"Do you?"

"I do."

"Say, Tommy, you make a mistake."

"I do?"

"Yes."

"How?"

"You appear to think that all those whom you dislike have to do is to stand up and be shot like deserters. Let me tell you something. Had you recognized me you would have been a dead man, that's all, and it is possible several of your pals might have gone the journey with you. It's better for you and them that you did not recognize me."

"The walls won't hold me long."

The detective laughed.

"When I am out I'll make it my business to settle you before I go back."

"Tommy, you surprise me."

"Do I?"

"Yes."

"How?"

"I thought you were a gamer man. Game men don't bark; you are barking."

"I'll bite; you did me up well; you've had your turn, I'll have mine."

"Yes, you'll get your turn. As far as I am concerned I don't care if you get out the day after you are sent up. I may have a chance then to do the state better service."

"You're barking now."

"No, I am only cautioning you, that's all. Tommy, I don't fear you."

A little later the party arrived at headquarters and the prisoner was turned over — one of the most dangerous rogues New York had known for a long time. The fellow had led a gang into a bank, had almost killed the watchman, had stolen over a hundred thousand dollars in money, and at least two hundred thousand more in negotiable securities, and he was a dangerous chap, and one of the most successful eluders the police had ever attempted to run down. Dudie Dunne had performed a great feat and yet he was to secure no public credit for it, for he was a secret special, and never in all his experience had he performed a deed that better earned him his right to be on the secret special force.

"How about the 'swag,' Dunne?"

"I don't expect to get it; but I am going back to look around."

"Better take some one with you."

"Not to-night — no, no."

Dunne returned to the place from which he had yanked his man. He entered by the door which he had left on the swing for the purpose of a second visit. Dunne ascended to the room from which he had carried his prize, and he commenced a search, and no burglar ever moved with greater noiselessness or ease. He was busy fully half an hour, going around with his tiny mask lantern, and finally there came a pleased look to his face. He drew a few instruments from his pocket and set to work, and soon he had removed several bricks from the chimney piece, and finding an aperture thrust in his hand and drew forth some bonds. He recovered all the securities, and about half the cash in bills of large denomination, and having completed his work he stole down the stairs and returned to headquarters, made his report and went off to his room for a few hours of genuine restful sleep.

On the morning following the incidents we have described the gang who had robbed him on the previous day assembled in the barroom. It was about eight o'clock, and as the last two came in they asked the man who was there ahead of them:

"Have you been up to take a peep?"

"No."

The men all laughed and one said:

"So you've heard nothing from our sweet little dude, eh?"

"No."

"Let's go up and take a peep at him and have a little fun; we will stand a heap of 'guying' when he awakes with his roaring headache."

The men with cheerful faces ascended the stairs. They opened the door and peeped in; the first man started back, his face pale, and he exclaimed:

"Great Scott!"

"What's the matter?"

"He's gone."

"Gone!" ejaculated the other two.

"Gone, as sure as guns, and rain storms."

The men passed into the room, then they all laughed.

The fools had not noticed until they commenced to laugh that they had found the door open. They really enjoyed the surprise for a moment until one of them suddenly appeared to fall to a suspicion.

"Hold on, fellows," he cried, "maybe we are laughing too soon. I don't understand this; come to think, if that chappie got out of here he wasn't as big a fool as we thought him."

"Oh, come off."

"I think we'd better go up and see Tommy — hear what he has to say."

The three men ascended to the room where the dude had gone for his game. They found that door open; they peeped in and Tommy was gone. He had disappeared, and they saw the opening where the "swag" had been secured. They looked into each other's faces and one of them said:

"This begins to look serious."

They descended to the barroom. The owner of the place had just appeared.

"Where is Tommy?" they demanded.

"Up in his room, of course."

"Is he?"

"Yes."

"Do you think he's there?"

"He is there."

"He is not."

"What?"

"He is not there."

"Where is he?"

"By all that's strange and miraculous, boys," cried the man who had first shot forth a suspicion, "we have been played. The dude was a 'copper,' and poor Tommy is in harbor at last."

The men sent out and got a paper, and the first head-line that met their eyes was:

"A Great Capture — Tom ——, the Worst Thief and Most Dangerous Bank Robber New York has Harbored for Many Years was Captured Last Night by a very Clever Piece of Detective Strategy and is Now at Police Headquarters."

The men trembled and one asked:

"What will we do?"

Another answered:

"I don't think the climate of New York agrees with me at this season of the year."

The others came to the same conclusion, and one said:

"We're in luck if we get away, but there is no time to lose."

The three men quietly glided from the saloon with countenances on which was written all evidences of terror.

CHAPTER III

A FEW WORDS AS TO THE REAL IDENTITY OF DUDIE DUNNE — THE DETECTIVE STARTS OUT ON A FRESH "LAY," AND AS A CHAPPIE SWEET CLOSES IN ON COMRADE NUMBER TWO.

There was nothing noteworthy in the career of Dudie or rather Oscar Dunne up to the time he entered upon the police force beyond the fact that he was of a very remarkable physical make-up. He was a young man possessed of very delicate features, girlish blue eyes and a clear red and white complexion. He was what is called a very effeminate-looking young man. We have seen others like him. We have previously alluded in this connection to two very striking examples similar to the case of Dudie Dunne, many years ago in New York. There were two men, both famous as athletes; one of them was noted as one of the most desperate rough-and-ready fighters in the city. He was a colonel in the late war, afterward a member of congress, and noted for his physical strength and daring, while he looked like a woman in the face, so delicate were his features, and so soft and fair his complexion. The other man was a notorious ring fighter, and he too possessed the same delicacy of feature and complexion, and yet was a man of wonderful physical strength. So with Oscar Dunne. He was pretty when a child and when a youth, and the boys nicknamed him

Girlie Dunne, and yet he outstripped all his boy companions in feats of strength and athletic performances. He was educated in the public schools of New York, and when quite young received an appointment as clerk to one of the city departments, and it was while acting in that capacity that he was led upon one occasion to attempt the running down of a notorious criminal. He tracked his man, had a desperate encounter with him, and captured him. This feat attracted attention toward him and one day a well-known detective remarked:

"Oscar, if I had your face and strength and nerve I'd become the greatest detective on earth."

Oscar brooded over the remark and later on secured a position on the regular police with a view to being promoted to the detective force, and his powers soon won him his promotion, and his services as a detective became so valuable, and his advantages as a detective became so marked, he was soon raised to the position of a secret special. It was just following his last promotion that he made the great capture we have recorded.

It was about a month following the incidents detailed when one day the chief sent for him and said:

"Oscar, I've a peculiar case for you. A great robbery was committed in Rome, Italy. Some very valuable heirlooms were stolen, besides a large collection of gems of great value. A large reward is offered for the thief, and it is believed by the Roman officers that the man is in New York."

"Did they send over a description?"

"No, they do not suspect any one man. All they suspect is that the thief fled from Rome and is in New York."

Oscar Dunne smiled as he remarked:

"A man must start on nothing in this case."

"That is about the size of it."

"They don't know whether the man is an Italian or not?"

"No, but they do know that he is a desperate fellow. He killed one of the servants in the house at the time he committed the robbery. They believe he is an Italian."

"Have you a photograph of any members of the family that was robbed?"

"No."

"Nor a photograph of the servant who was murdered."

"No."

Oscar was thoughtful a moment and then said:

"Chief, a man who is blindfolded in a dark room can't see a crack in the wall."

"Hardly."

"There are thousands upon thousands of Italians in New York."

"Yes."

"And many of them are hard characters — desperate fellows."

"You are right. But there are a great many excellent Italians in New York — men of the highest character and integrity."

"I know that."

"They will aid you."

"How can they aid me? Italy is a very big country. I'd look foolish merely to tell them that a robbery had been committed in Rome and that I wanted to find out something about it."

"What do you want?"

"I want something to start on."

"The Roman police have given us all they can."

"They haven't given us anything."

"Then you think it's no use to start in?"

"I didn't say so. If the man is in New York I'll find him, but I must have something to work on."

"I don't know what I can give you."

"I want a photograph of every member of the family that was robbed. I want a photograph of the servant that was killed, and then I want certain questions answered direct from the family."

"We will have to send to Italy."

"Good enough. I will prepare my questions at once. You can send to Rome for what I want, and in the meantime I will be looking around. It will take about three weeks or a month for us to get a return from Rome. By that time I may have something to start out on, at least a subject for the working of the plan I may form after I hear from Rome."

"I see your point, Oscar; it's well taken."

Dudie Dunne prepared the questions he wished answered and started out for a little tour of observation. He was gotten up as the dude, but he had half a dozen different types of the dude with which he alternated in getting up his disguise. He also was able when occasion required to work the female racket as a cover beyond any other man who had ever attempted the role.

There was one feature of Dudie Dunne's disguises. He acted the character he assumed. He never lost his head or forgot himself, and going around as he did under the guise of one of the most harmless of mortals, he had excellent chances for getting information. Under the fleece of the lamb was the hide of the lion, and there was just where he came in when the crisis was presented. Oscar was standing on the corner of a street waiting for a car to pass when he saw a man suddenly leap off the car, and immediately afterward an old lady ran out to the platform screaming, "Stop thief! stop thief!"

The conductor did not even stop the car, but Dudie was at hand. He made a leap forward, only a leap, for the thief ran close to him, and he seized the rascal, when immediately a second man who had jumped off the car ran up while Oscar was struggling with the thief. The second man proved a confederate of the first, and he grabbed hold of Oscar. There was no policeman near, but a crowd had gathered and the people merely looked on, not understanding the cause of the struggle. They thought it was great fun, and one of the crowd created a laugh by yelling:

"Hang on to him, chappie; hang on to him."

Well, he did not hang on to him — he did better. Thief number two had hauled off to deal Oscar a tremendous blow. He was a large man and appeared to possess great strength, but to the surprise of everybody, chappie, as the crowd had dubbed our hero, let go the man he had been holding just in time to dodge a blow aimed at his head, and he countered with a stinger which sent his assailant staggering to the street. He then as quick as a wink, to the amazement of the crowd, dealt the man he had first seized a sockdologer and down he went, and at the same instant the old lady arrived on the scene. She had beheld the capture and saw the thief knocked out. The crowd cheered at the powers of chappie when the truth went flying around that the two men whom the chappie downed were pickpockets, and that the old lady was their victim. Our hero followed his man and took from him quick as lightning the purse which the thief had slid to his bosom. This he handed to the old lady, who quickly disappeared, and at the same instant a policeman arrived. The thief was a quickwitted fellow and he said:

"Arrest that man. He just robbed an old lady of her

pocketbook."

Oscar did appear most like a thief and the policeman seized him.

"Hold on, officer, there's your man," said Oscar, pointing to the retreating thief.

"Oh, you can't play that on me," said the officer, and he commenced without further inquiry to cuff his prisoner over the head in a very rough manner, when suddenly the dude wrested himself clear and let the officer have one on the ear, and then the crowd laughed and jeered as the cop went reeling. Another officer arrived on the field. He also happened to be a fresh Alec. He didn't stop to ask a question but drew his club and made a rush at the supposed thief; the latter had no time to make an explanation. It was take a knock on the head or fight. He decided to fight and explain afterward, so he let "copper" number two have one, and it did appear marvelous, the ease with which he dropped the knights of the brass buttons. Cop number one had regained his feet, and drawing his club was about to make a rush, when Oscar threw back the lapel of his coat, and the officer's eyes rested on a little silver badge that caused him to recoil as though he had been confronted by a ghost.

Both policemen fell to their blunder and the detective said:

"Go and hunt up your right men now and don't be so fast next time."

Assuming his chappie walk our hero ambled away. On the following morning there appeared an account in the papers, telling how a detective, very smartly dressed, had knocked out and captured two pickpockets when a policeman came along and mistaking the detective for the thief permitted the real thief to depart.

A day or two passed when our hero, who made a

daily practice to look over the personals in all the journals, saw a little advertisement which read as follows:

"If the detective who recovered an old lady's pocket-book will send his address to Mrs. I. F., Station B, he will hear of something to his advantage."

"Well," ejaculated the officer, "that means me. Now let us see — what shall we do?"

It did not take the detective very long to decide upon his course. He wrote the letter, and proceeding to Station B, mailed it, then he lay around for several hours until he saw a very nice-looking young lady call and ask for a letter addressed to "I. F." The letter was delivered and the girl started off with the detective on her track. He trailed her to an old-fashioned house in a very excellent neighborhood.

The girl meantime entered the house and delivered the letter to an old lady — the same old lady who had been robbed. The latter said, as the girl entered the room to the left of the hall:

"What! you have an answer already?"

"Yes, aunty."

The old woman took the letter, opened it and read:

"Madam: I saw your advertisement. I will call upon you. When a card is presented with the name of the undersigned you will know it is the detective.

"Yours,

"Oscar Dunne."

"Well, I declare," exclaimed the old lady; "he will call on us."

"But how will he know where to call, aunty; you did not give your address in the advertisement."

"That is so. I had forgotten that. Why, how will he know where to call. I fear I have made a mistake. A man who is as big a dunce as that can be of no service to us."

"But wait, aunty, these men sometimes have dark and mysterious ways of their own for finding out facts. Let's wait and see if he does call."

Even as the girl spoke there came a ring at the door bell, and a few minutes later a servant presented a card on which was the name, "Oscar Dunne."

"Why, Alice, he is here; it's wonderful."

"Will you see him?"

"Yes."

"Alone?"

"Yes, retire, my child."

The niece retired and a few moments later Oscar was ushered into the old lady's presence.

CHAPTER IV

DUDIE DUNNE LISTENS TO A STRANGE STORY AND ENTERS UPON A TRAIL THAT LEADS TO MANY VERY STARTLING ADVENTURES.

"I am surprised to see you here."

"Is that so, madam?"

"Yes."

"Why should you be when you expressed a desire to see me?"

"When did I express such a desire?"

"The desire was implied in your advertisement."

"But I did not put my address in the advertisement. How did you establish my identity?"

The detective smiled and said:

"It was a very simple matter, madam."

"I do not understand it."

"I will explain."

"Please do."

"We detectives are compelled to be very careful in all our movements. We have enemies who are constantly seeking to trap us."

"What has all that to do with the fact that you knew my address?"

"I read your advertisement."

"Yes."

"I did not know whether it was genuine or a decoy

sent out by the thieves who robbed you."

"But even that does not explain how you obtained my address."

"By a very simple plan, madam."

"Tell me your plan."

"I mailed the letter to you."

"Yes."

"I knew you would send a messenger for it."

"Certainly."

"I lay around the post office for your messenger. When she came I followed her here."

"Oh, I see; well, how stupid I am. It is evident I am not a female detective. I never should have thought of that expedient."

"It is a very simple one. If it had been a trap the parties sending the letter would have taken precautions not to be trapped that way."

"I see, yes, I see; well, you are not a dunce after all."

"Thank you. You wished to see me?"

"Yes."

"Madam, what is your name, please?"

"My name is Mrs. Frewen."

"Who is the young lady who called for the answer to the advertisement?"

"My niece."

"And her name?"

"Alice Frewen. She is my brother's daughter. She is an orphan."

"You wished to see me on business?"

"Yes."

"Why did you send for me?"

"I will tell you. I read in the papers that you were a detective. I saw your bold act in catching the thief who had robbed me, and a little incident occurred that suggested to me that I had better consult with a detective. I had beheld your gallant action and my niece suggested the plan of the advertisement for your employment."

"Very well, madam; on what business do you desire to consult me about?"

The old lady produced a letter which read:

"Dear Madam: You are in danger. Remove all the portable valuables from your house; leave nothing around that thieves can carry away.
    A Friend."

The detective read and re-read the missive and finally asked in a simple sort of way:

"Who sent this, madam?"

"You see the signature."

"A friend."

"That is all I know."

"Can you form the least idea as to who this friend, or rather this so-called friend is? Have you the least suspicion as to his identity?"

"I have not."

"Has your niece?"

"No."

"This letter would suggest that there is a scheme on foot to rob you."

"That is the suggestion that came to me when I first read the note."

"Have you any articles of special value in the house?"

"You are a detective."

"I am."

"I believe your identity and respectability are sufficiently well established for me to answer you frankly."

"Madam, you can reserve your answer if you choose

until you thoroughly establish my identity and respectability."

"It is not necessary. I am satisfied. Yes, I have articles of special value in this house."

"Who would be likely to know the fact?"

"No one beyond my niece."

"You cannot think of any one who would be apt to know that you had articles of special value in the house?"

"No."

"Is there any one whom you suspect of wishing to scare you?"

"No, the fact is we have no acquaintances in New York. We have lived abroad many years and only returned to New York about six months ago. This house came to me by inheritance. It was leased for ten years to a family whom I never knew. My agent leased it. It stood idle for six months, until I came and reopened it upon my return home about six months ago."

"When you were abroad where did you reside principally?"

"In Paris; my niece attended school in France."

"I suppose you had a great many friends in Paris?"

"No, very few; I am not of a social turn at all. I do not seek friends. I live a very secluded life for reasons which it is not necessary to explain."

"Then there are none of your Paris friends whom you would suspect as the author of that warning note?"

"No."

The detective re-read the note, examined it very carefully, and finally said:

"We can form no suspicion from the note itself."

"No."

"Madam, have you an album?"

"Yes."

"Will you let me look at it?"

"For what purpose?"

"I wish to look at the pictures of some of the people you knew in Paris."

The old lady smiled and said:

"The album belongs to my niece. It is merely a collection of prominent French characters — public men, statesmen, army officers, musicians, painters and actors — the photographs do not represent friends of ours."

"Still you have no objection to my seeing it?"

"No, sir."

"Please let me see it, and if you have no objection let your niece be present. She may recall facts that have possibly slipped from your memory."

"You are a very strange young man."

"Yes, I am a very strange young man and I go about my business in a strange manner. Madam, you did the right thing when you sent for me. You and your niece are two lone ladies living in this house. It is evident some one has discovered that you have valuables in your house. A scheme of robbery, it would appear from the warning note, is contemplated. Some one friendly to you has learned of the intended robbery and has warned you. This warning may not only save your property but your life, and it is necessary that we should make every effort to learn who sent the warning note. I desire to see the photographs."

Mrs. Frewen summoned her niece and requested her to bring her photograph album. The niece entered the room and was introduced to our hero, and she failed to conceal her surprise upon being informed that the handsome young man, so exquisitely attired, was a celebrated and successful detective. If Oscar noted her surprise he did not indicate it, but took the album and deliberately commenced turning over its pages, and the niece standing over him said:

"You will only find pictures of well-known characters in the album. I do not think there is a photograph of a single friend of ours in the book."

"Then you have another book?"

"No."

"You do not keep pictures of your friends?"

"No."

"It is unfortunate under the present circumstances; but, miss, what public character is the original of that photograph?"

The girl blushed and answered:

"I had forgotten that the picture was in the album."

"Ah, I see; but who is the original?"

"Oh, he is a young man whose mother I knew in Paris. Aunty was very kind to the mother and also to the young man at the time he was sick."

"Did you ever see this young man?"

"Never."

"Did your aunt ever see him?"

"Yes, she remained with the mother one or two nights, aiding in nursing him, and she supported them during his illness."

"What created your aunt's interest in the young man?"

"His mother had been her maid many years previously."

"What is the character of the young man?"

The girl did not answer.

"You do not answer me."

"It is a very singular question."

"It is?"

"Yes."

"How?"

"I never saw the young man, how should I know anything concerning his character?"

Mrs. Frewen had been an interested listener to the conversation, and turning to the aunt our hero said:

"You know this young man?"

"Yes."

"He is a very handsome young fellow, I should think, from his picture."

"Yes, and a very unfortunate young man."

"Unfortunate?"

"Yes."

"In what way — simply because his mother was poor?"

"No, there is a mystery connected with his life."

"A mystery?"

"Yes."

"What is the mystery?"

"I believe his father is a nobleman, although his mother was my governess."

"Ah, your governess?"

"Yes."

"Not your maid?"

"She acted as governess and maid both. She was a very handsome woman. We were in Italy when she eloped and ran away."

"Did she run away and get married?"

"She claimed she was married."

"Whom did she marry?"

"She would never reveal the man's identity."

"Do you know that it was a nobleman?"

"No."

"You only suspect?"

"Yes."

"What led you to the suspicion."

"Hints that Madam Donetti dropped from time to time."

"This young man's name is Donetti?"

"He is known as Alphonse Donetti."

"An Italian name."

"Yes."

"Then you conclude his mother married an Italian?"

"Yes."

"Was he a sober, industrious young man?"

"No, he appeared to feel very much embittered at the idea of being poor. He claimed to be of high birth. Indeed I have suspected that his mother was a woman descended from a good old French family; at any rate the young man is very high-blooded, fond of gay life, and unable to gratify his desires."

"Did he ever to your knowledge commit a crime?"

"Never to my knowledge."

"Did you ever hear it whispered that he was a criminal?"

The old lady did not answer.

"You do not answer me."

"I fear he caused his mother a great deal of anxiety at times."

"His mother still resides in France?"

"She is dead."

"Where is the young man?"

"I don't know."

"Where did you see him last?"

"In Paris."

"How long ago?"

"About a year ago."

"When and where?"

"I saw him upon the street."

"Did you address him?"

"No."

"Why not?"

The woman did not answer.

"Please answer me."

"He was in the hands of a sergeant de ville."

"He was under arrest?"

"Yes."

"For what offense?"

"I never inquired, and the day following my niece and I started for London."

"You have no reason to suspect that Alphonse Donetti is in the United States, in fact in New York?"

"The suggestion did not arise in my mind until you began to question me about him, then I did ask myself the question: Could it have been Alphonse Donetti who sent me that warning note?"

The detective meditated a long time and then said:

"The chances are that Alphonse Donetti sent you that warning note."

"I cannot think who else could have sent it, and yet I have no knowledge that he is in the United States."

"The note is written in good English."

"Yes, Alphonse was educated in England; his mother devoted her life to him, and as long as she had a cent she denied him nothing. All her money was spent when she came to me, and I aided her."

"And Alphonse knew of your generosity to his mother?"

"Yes."

"And she married an Italian?"

"I believe it was an Italian with whom she eloped. We were living in Florence at the time. She deserted me and ran away."

"And you did not see her until many years afterward?"

"No."

"And then you met her in Paris?"

"Yes."

"Was Donetti her married name?"

"I have every reason to believe it was an assumed name. I firmly believe she eloped with some man of high family, even though he may not have been a nobleman, but I believe he was a nobleman."

"You say Madam Donetti was a handsome young lady?"

"Very handsome — a beautiful woman and refined, also highly educated. There was a mystery about her while she was acting as my governess."

"Governess to whom — yourself?"

"No, an older sister of Alice."

"She was a Frenchwoman?"

"I always believed so, but as she assumed the name of Donetti it is possible she may have been Italian, or her parents may have been Italian people."

"She spoke Italian?"

"She did indeed. She spoke all the continental languages, also English, and her son is a splendid linguist."

"Madam, that note came from Alphonse Donetti."

"And what does it portend?"

The detective meditated a few moments and then said:

"I can only theorize."

"And what is your theory?"

"I fear Alphonse has gotten into bad company. I fear he is associating with thieves. He may have learned that there was a scheme on foot to rob you. He did not dare warn you fully, but sent you this missive, and the fact that he sent you this note would indicate that no matter how bad a man he has become he still possesses the quality of gratitude. A very rare quality, madam; few possess it. Forgetfulness and selfishness prevail as a rule."

"What are we to do?"

"Will you leave the decision with me?"

"Certainly."

"We will guard against a robbery, and in the meantime I will hunt up this young man Donetti; if he is in New York I will find him."

Mrs. Frewen meditated a few moments in turn and then said:

"I do not know as I wish to renew his acquaintance, especially as he has probably become a criminal."

Oscar smiled, but the smile on his face vanished as he caught an expression on the face of the niece Alice as she said:

"Aunty, we have no reason to assume that Al — I mean the young man has become a criminal."

The girl started to say Alphonse but checked herself and said, "the young man."

Oscar was a regular mind-reader, and he remarked in a tone indicating a forgetfulness that the question had once been answered:

"So you never had the pleasure of seeing this young man, Miss Alice?"

The girl blushed and appeared restless and uneasy as she answered:

"No."

The detective turned to Mrs. Frewen and said:

"It may be necessary to hunt up this young man in order to run down the criminals who, we are to assume, are about to make an attempt to rob you."

"I fear the young man is a criminal."

"But, aunty, he is very considerate when he warns us."

"Yes, he owes it to me, and I am glad he evidently possesses at least one good quality; but I fear his deeds were the death of his mother. She did not reveal to me all she knew about her son, that is evident, and now under the new light I can see clearly and interpret many little incidents that before I could not understand."

"I will ask to borrow this picture, madam."

"You can take it," said the elder lady, but the younger one said:

"No, no, aunty, do not let the gentleman have the picture."

"Why not, my child?"

"Well, it is better that he does not discover the young man. In case his theories are correct it might lead to mortifying incidents. We do not know the young man, and probably it is better that we let him drop from our memories forever."

"I will see that no complications arise from the discovery of the young man. If he is a criminal who has come over here from France it may be as well to cut him short in his career of crime on this side of the ocean as quickly as possible."

"And what would you do?"

"It is my duty to note every criminal as far as I can, and run him down if he makes himself answerable to our laws."

"You have no proof that this young man is a criminal."

"No, I have no proof, but I am satisfied that he is a criminal, and it is possible I can already associate him with a very grave crime."

The face of Alice became ghastly as her aunt asked:

"Alice, why do you show such interest in this criminal?"

"Aunty, I only show the interest that is natural, considering the esteem in which you held his mother."

The keen eyes of the detective were on the girl and he reached a very startling conclusion, and other very strange and startling suggestions and suspicions were running through his mind.

"I will take the photograph," he said, "and will guarantee no unpleasant incidents will follow my possession of it; and now, madam, one more point — I will come to your house to-night between eleven o'clock and midnight and remain here as a private watchman in order to anticipate the visit of the burglars in case a raid on your house is meditated."

"I am glad to have you do so, and I will have a room prepared for you, and I will pay you according to what you may think your services demand."

CHAPTER V

DUDIE DUNNE LAYS LOW FOR THE HOUSEBREAKERS, MAKES A GREAT CAPTURE, AND ALSO MAKES A VERY PECULIAR DISCOVERY.

The detective completed his arrangements for spending a night in the house. He also gave instructions to Mrs. Frewen and her niece just what they were to do under the possibilities of the approaching night. A little later and the detective took his departure, and still later met the chief, to whom he said:

"Strange incidents meet us in our profession, chief."

"Well, I should say so. What have you struck now?"

"I am not sure, chief, but I've an idea that I have run by accident right on to the Roman burglar. If I have it's the most extraordinary chance that ever occurred in our profession."

Oscar proceeded and related to the chief what had occurred. The latter listened and said:

"I don't see where the Roman robbery comes in."

"You don't?"

"No."

"Well, you've been busy, and your mind is not clear."

"I feel pretty clear in my head."

Oscar opened up the key to his theory and the chief exclaimed:

"Dudie, you're a genius. By all that's strange and

wonderful I should not be amazed if you are right, and do you know there is the biggest sort of a reward offered for the capture of the thief."

"Chief, if my ideas are fully confirmed we may not seek the reward. I don't know but my suspicions run a great way in this case, and if the fact proves true — well, we'll talk it over after we locate, identify and prove the crime on our man."

It was just about eleven o'clock when Dudie Dunne turned the corner to go to the house where he was to spend the night. He was walking along lost in a brown study when suddenly a hand was laid lightly upon his shoulder. He turned and beheld a veiled woman.

Now, reader, don't exclaim, "There comes one of Old Sleuth's veiled women again," for I tell you veiled women are floating around every day and night in great cities, and especially those who, like our veiled women, are out at such a late hour on special business.

"Can I have a few words with you, Mr. Dunne?" came the question.

"Great Scott!" thought our hero, but the exclamation did not escape his lips.

"Certainly, Miss Alice," he answered.

"I can rely upon your honor that what passes between us shall be strictly confidential?"

"Yes, miss."

"You will not even reveal the fact that I met you?"

"I will not, but will not your aunt miss you?"

"No, she retired over an hour ago. She is a heavy sleeper; even the prospect of a visit from burglars would not keep her awake as long as the prospect was only a suspicion. She is a very brave lady; my aunt is a very remarkable woman."

"No doubt; but now what can I do for you?"

"A crisis compels me to be singularly frank with you."

"It is better so if I am to serve you in any way."

"I am about to make an extraordinary request."

"All right."

"It is possible those burglars may visit our house to-night."

"Yes, it is possible, not probable. I tell you now I am only exercising due precaution, I do not really anticipate a visit from the housebreakers."

"I do."

"You have a reason for your conclusion?"

"I have."

"What is it?"

"Never mind; but I wish to make a request."

"Proceed."

"If the robbers do enter our house, the moment you spring upon them they will attempt to escape of course."

"That will naturally be what they will attempt, I should say."

"If you surprise them they will be defeated."

"Certainly."

"They will not have taken anything."

"Possibly not."

"Then let them escape."

"That is your request?"

"Yes."

"It is indeed a very singular one."

"I cannot explain why I make such a request, but please let them escape. I repeat I cannot explain why I make the request."

"You cannot explain why you make such a strange request?"

"No."

"You need not."

"Thank you, and I am to understand that my request is granted?"

"Oh, no."

"What do you mean?"

"I mean you need not make any explanation, that is all."

The girl stared. Our hero could not see her eyes, for she was veiled, but her attitude indicated that she was staring at him and he knew with a look of surprise on her face.

"Why do you not seek an explanation of such an extraordinary request?"

"Simply because it is really unnecessary. I know why you make the request. I fully comprehend your motive."

An exclamation escaped the veiled lady.

"You understand?"

"I do."

"No, no, it is impossible that you understand."

"I will prove to you that I do understand. You fear that Alphonse Donetti will be one of the burglars. You do not desire him to be captured. See what a mind-reader I am."

"Why do you assume that Alphonse will be one of the robbers?"

"Merely because you do, that's all."

"How do you know that I do?"

"You would not make the extraordinary request unless that was your fear."

"You are a strange man."

The detective laughed and answered:

"And you are a very strangely acting lady. It is indeed a strange thing for a lady who expects robbers to visit her house to ask that they be permitted to escape. I must do my duty, miss, I cannot grant your request unless you ask that I let Alphonse go and arrest the others."

"No, that will not do," she exclaimed, "for the others would betray him."

"Aha!" ejaculated the detective, "human-like you have given yourself away. Do not again deny your real motive for making the request."

The girl recognized that indeed she had betrayed herself, and in a tone of distress she muttered:

"Oh, what shall I do?"

"I can tell you."

"Please do."

"Make a full confidant of me."

"Will you believe me?"

"I know of no reason why I should doubt your word."

"I have already deceived you."

"Eh! you have already deceived me?"

"I have."

"In what direction?"

"I told you I had never seen or spoken to Alphonse Donetti?"

"I remember."

"My denial was false."

The detective was silent.

"I did not dare let my aunt know that I had ever seen him."

"And you have met?"

"Yes."

"Often?"

"Yes, very often. He has confided in me."

"One moment! are you his affianced wife?"

"On my honor, I am not; but knowing his real story I sympathize with him most heartily."

"He has revealed to you more than his mother ever revealed to your aunt?"

"Yes."

"Tell me what he revealed to you."

"I cannot."

"Oh, but you can."

"No, I am bound by an oath; I cannot break my oath."

The detective meditated and then asked:

"Do you know that Donetti is in New York?"

"I do not."

"Have you reason to suspect that he is?"

"I had no reason to so suspect until you indicated that he was possibly the author of the warning note, then I did suspect that he was in New York."

"Have you any grounds for believing that he is a criminal?"

"I have not."

"Then why do you fear he may be with the robbers to-night?"

"I do not know to what desperate deeds his many wrongs and privations may have driven him. If he is in New York I will find him. If he is being driven toward the career of a criminal I will save him. If you arrest him I cannot save him, and yet he deserves to be saved, for he is the victim of a great wrong."

Again the detective meditated. He was revolving strange theories in his mind, and mentally he concluded: "This is a very unfortunate girl, but she is only one of a type of woman who can be thus fascinated." After an interval he said:

"I do not think Alphonse will be one of the robbers."

"You believe he is in New York?"

"Yes, I believe so."

"How would he know of the intended robbery?"

"That is a question I cannot answer. Indeed I can

advance no theory, but I do not believe he will be one of the robbers."

"It is possible he is not in New York at all."

"Yes, it is possible, but the probabilities are that he is."

Alice appeared very unhappy, and our hero could not console her with a promise, simply because he had reason to believe that Alphonse Donetti was possibly already liable to arrest for a previous crime.

"You can give me no comfort?" she said at length.

"No, beyond the fact that I will agree to let Alphonse escape in case he is among the burglars who may possibly enter your house."

"And the others will betray him."

"No, you need not fear that; but time passes, I must go and take up my position. You had better return to your home and I will appear later."

The girl slowly walked away and our hero muttered:

"Well, this is a complication. That girl loves a thief, possibly an assassin."

A little later and Oscar Dunne entered the house. All was as it had been agreed it should be, and yet the detective commenced a search. There was a hall pantry off the rear parlor. The detective tried the door; it was locked, but by a little trick of his own he opened it and flashed the light of his tiny mask lantern inside, and there sure enough stood Alice Frewen. The girl colored, but assumed a very defiant look as she said:

"You had no business to force yourself into my room."

"Your room is of very narrow dimensions, but under the circumstances I was compelled to force my way in as I wish to use this room as my hiding place, and further I do not propose that you shall give the burglars warning. I am here to catch them and I will."

"Never; I will warn them. I will light the gas and sit up all night."

"Oh, you will?"

"Yes."

"Do not resolve upon so rash a proceeding."

"I shall do as I threaten."

"I am sorry, but I shall be compelled to arouse your aunt and inform her of your intention; also as an explanation, reveal to her all that you have revealed to me."

The girl burst into tears and exclaimed:

"I am at your mercy; what shall I do?"

"I'll tell you what to do."

"Please tell me."

"Trust me. Trust my judgment and consideration for your feelings."

"Let me explain."

"Yes, you are at liberty to explain."

"I wish to save that young man simply because I believe he is the victim of a great wrong. I do not believe he is bad at heart — not a criminal by nature."

"I will not question your motive, but you cannot interfere with the performance of my duty, but I will promise you that no harm shall come to the young man until I am convinced that he is an irreclaimable villain. If he is the victim of wrong he shall have my aid and sympathy. I can promise you no more than that, beyond the assurance that I am sincere, and I know just what to do."

"I will trust you."

"You are wise."

"You will keep my secret?"

"As long as you obey my instructions."

"I will obey your instructions."

"Then retire to your room and do not come forth

until I summon you, or you are summoned by your aunt."

The girl ascended the stairs and our hero prepared for a night's vigil. He was acting, as he stated, merely as a matter of precaution. He did not anticipate the advent of the burglars, but he was just as watchful and careful as though he knew for a certainty that they would come. He did not sleep, but lay down on a sofa in the rear parlor, raising the two windows so as to overhear any noise in case the thieves should put in an appearance. He knew the habits of the robbers well enough. He knew how their methods would be adapted to the lay of the house they were to enter. The house was detached, and there was a storm shed in the rear protecting the back kitchen door. Here was where he anticipated they would make their entrance. Once in the storm shed they could take their time in opening the kitchen door, and could also make all their arrangements for escape in case of discovery.

The hours passed until about three o'clock in the morning, when the detective, who despite all his doubts had been on the alert, heard a sound. He peeped out, and there sure enough he beheld three men in the yard, and he muttered:

"By ginger! they are here. Well, I didn't expect them, but I will welcome them."

Dudie Dunne was a very resolute young man. He wore moccasins and with noiseless tread passed to the kitchen stairway and there took up his position. He knew the men would advance by the stairs the moment they succeeded in getting into the house. Holding his position he waited, and was not surprised at the celerity of their movements, for within ten minutes after his first recognition of their presence in the yard he had evidence that they were in the house — and there he stood at the head of the kitchen stairs prepared to lay them out.

The men were old hands at the business. They wasted no time, but started to ascend the kitchen stairs just as Oscar had calculated they would. He lay low until the foremost man was just at the last step, when a club cut the air; there followed a thud and an outcry and the man went over backward upon the man who was following him.

The detective leaned down the stairs. He stepped over the man he had struck and arrived at the foot of the stairs just as robber number two had risen to his feet, having been knocked down by his pal's fall. Again the club cut the air and robber number two received a clip that disabled him and the detective sprang along to the kitchen. Robber number three had been on the watch. He knew some thing had gone wrong and ran to the kitchen to hear what had occurred. He arrived just in time to run up against that effective club, and he too went down, and as he fell the detective leaped upon him and fixed the darbies on him. He then retired to the basement hall stairs, and arrived just as number two had a second time risen to his feet; the man received a second dose from the club and went down again, and in less time than it takes to record it the darbies were run on him. Robber number one had not moved; the blow he had received had sort of settled him for a little rest, but the detective put the steel bands on him all the same, and then he turned on the gas. None of the burglars had masks on, although they had their little face-hiders hanging to their lapels like a pair of eyeglasses.

Oscar went to each man and flashed the light of his lantern in their faces one after the other, and then he muttered:

"Well, he is not here; so far so good."

The detective went to the front door and swung his light, and in less than two minutes two men appeared. They were admitted and led down to the kitchen where they seized the robbers. Our hero had recognized two of the men. They were the fellows who had played him for a "chappie."

The three burglars were led through the kitchen door to the yard and marched off, three of the most surprised housebreakers that were ever captured; and right here we have a word to say. There is nothing romantic and daring in housebreaking. It is one of the most atrocious crimes on the criminal calendar. It is simply terrible to think of people defenseless and helpless in their own homes and beds when masked men, prepared to do murder, steal in to rob them. There is no palliation for this offense, for there is no crime, save that of forgery, that is conducted with so much forethought, decision and calculation — yes, calculation to do murder if it becomes necessary, for they go prepared to kill; and it is a grand thing when one of these cruel scoundrels is caught and punished. They are not entitled to sympathy, despite the fact that some mawkish Sunday-school books some-times present the good-hearted burglar. If there is any crime that deserves death anywhere near the liability of murder it is the crime of burglary, for a man who will enter a house to steal is the meanest criminal on the face of the earth, and it is well when they are shot down right in their tracks and in the act of their crime.

The three burglars, as stated, were led away, and our hero, who had effected the capture so neatly, ascended the stairs and at the parlor door met Alice Frewen.

"They have been here."

"You have disobeyed me."

"I did not until I knew it was all over."

"Did you know it was all over?"

"Yes."

"How?"

"I was watching and listening."

"Well, they did come. I did not expect them, I will admit."

"You have captured them?"

"Yes."

"All of them?"

"Yes."

"Did you see their faces?"

"I did."

"And —"

"*He* was not among them."

"You are sure?"

"I am sure."

"Remember, he may have been under a disguise."

"He was not with them. I recognized all the three men. I know them. No, he was not with them, and the chances are all our theories were wrong, but we will learn later on."

CHAPTER VI

DUDIE DUNNE STARTS OUT ON A QUEST AND ENCOUNTERS SOME VERY CURIOUS ADVENTURES, TOGETHER WITH SEVERAL RUN-INS WITH MEN WHO TAKE HIM FOR A CHAPPIE.

The girl Alice appeared to be greatly relieved and retired to her room while our hero lay down on the sofa and slept. He needed some rest and was glad of the opportunity to secure it.

On the following morning he saw Mrs. Frewen. That good lady had slept along undisturbed while the exciting incidents we have recorded were transpiring. Our hero related to her all that had occurred, and she said:

"Well, you are a very faithful man, and I desire a confidential talk with you."

Mrs. Frewen and the detective were in the rear sitting-room. The old lady closed the door and said in a low tone:

"What I say to you is purely confidential."

"All right, madam."

"You captured the burglars?"

"I did."

"You saw their faces?"

"I did."

"Plainly enough to identify them in case you had known them?"

"Yes."

"Did you recognize any of them?"

"I recognized them all."

"You did?"

"I did."

"Well?"

"What is it you want to know?"

"Was *he* among them?"

"Who?"

"The young man Alphonse Donetti?"

"No."

There came a disappointed look to the old lady's face and she said:

"I am sorry."

"You are sorry, madam."

"Yes, I am sorry."

"Why?"

"I have no confidence in that young man."

"Do you know that he is in New York?"

"I do not know, but I suspect that he is."

"And you wanted him captured as a burglar?"

"Yes."

"After he sent you the warning note?"

"Yes."

The detective was silent, but there came a curious expression to his face.

"It may appear strange to you."

"Yes."

"I can trust you?"

"Yes."

"Yesterday I made a discovery, or rather you made one for me."

"I did?"

"Yes."

"How?"

"By the finding of that photograph in that album. I have long suspected a certain fact, now I have evidence that there are grounds for my suspicions."

"Will you speak plainly, madam?"

"I will."

"Do so."

"Again I ask, can I trust you?"

"You can."

"In a matter purely personal?"

"Yes."

"Then I will declare that I have reason to suspect that the rascal, Alphonse Donetti, has fascinated my niece, and I fear the girl has been deliberately deceiving me."

Our hero made no comment, and the old lady continued:

"At the terror of fearing that my own flesh and blood has been fascinated by a thief — in my opinion a born thief — the son of a thief — a low, vile, reckless scoundrel, yes, that is what I fear. It was this suspicion that caused me to leave Paris. And now, Oscar Dunne, you can make your fortune. I am a very rich woman; I can pay a great price. I want you to aid me to save my niece, even if she is compelled to gaze on the dead face of her lover."

"Madam, what do you mean? Can you believe that money will tempt me to commit a murder?"

"No, sir, I am not a murderess, but I believe money will induce you to bring a murderer to justice, and have him hung as he deserves."

"Well," thought the detective, "here is a pretty kettle of fish right in one family."

"Madam, are you sure you have made a discovery?"

"Yes, I have other evidences. What I learned yesterday was only confirmatory."

"I see you are disposed to trust me."

"Yes."

"Let me say for myself that your confidence is not displaced, and if you have reason to believe that your niece is in love with a criminal, and if we prove the man to be a criminal, I will aid you in removing the human toy beyond her reach. I will send him up to the gallows."

"Well, now, you are assuming that he is a murderer."

"I have every reason to believe that he is, and I think the evidence can be secured to convict him; but why should he seek to marry your niece?"

"He knows she is an heiress — yes, a great heiress. She is heir to millions, and will have the money in her own right without any restraint upon her use or misuse of it whatever."

"When?"

"When she becomes of age."

"How old is she now?"

"In about three years she will come into absolute possession of her fortune."

"And this man, you think, has bewitched her?"

"I do."

"And yet she denied ever having met him."

"I know it, and I will say this in her favor; she is a noble and truthful girl. She believes that wretch innocent. She thinks I am unwarrantably prejudiced, and that under the circumstances it is not wrong to deceive me. She thinks he is a wronged young man. She has been assailed on a woman's weakest side — her sympathies."

"Have you positive evidence that the young man is the villain you believe him to be?"

"Not positive evidence, not convicting evidence; that is what I want you to obtain."

"Is it not possible that your niece is right?"

"Right!" almost screamed Mrs. Frewen.

"Yes."

"Right, how?"

"Is it not possible that the young man has been wronged and is innocent?"

"No, she is not right. He is guilty, and you must obtain the proofs, and I will pay you an enormous reward."

"Madam, I will try and earn the reward, and in order to do so you must tell me what evidence you have of this young man's guilt."

"I have no evidence."

"You have no evidence?"

"No actual evidence."

"On what do you found your suspicions?"

"His general character."

"What is his general character?"

"I don't know positively. All I know is what I have heard and general rumor."

"One more question. Have you any evidence that he is in America?"

"Here again I have no evidence, but there are certain circumstances that point conclusively to the fact that he is in New York."

"And do you believe he sent you the warning note?"

"I do."

"What could have been his object?"

"Oh, it was a cunning trick on his part. He is making evidence, that's all."

"Making evidence?"

"Yes."

"To establish what?"

"That he is a pure young man and has been wronged. I really believed he would be with the burglars. You are to establish the fact that he instigated the robbery, that these men are his pals, as you detectives call them, and you are to follow him up and establish his career as a professional thief and criminal."

"I must find him first."

"Yes, you must find him, and I think you will succeed. You have his photograph; it is an excellent picture; when she got it I don't know, and I tell you it was hard for me to dissimulate yesterday, but I do not desire her to know that I suspect, even when we have all the proofs, and want it to come as a revelation to her. I never wish her to know that I ever suspected the truth."

"Madam, I will undertake to establish the fact that this young man is a criminal, or the victim of cruel suspicions."

"He is a criminal, I am sure of it."

"One moment; do you wish it to be established that he is a criminal, whether he is or not?"

The detective fixed a keen look on Mrs. Frewen's face as he asked the question. A moment the old lady hesitated and then said:

"Yes."

Promptly the detective answered:

"Under these circumstances, madam, you will have to secure the services of another person."

"But do not forget your reward."

"Madam, all your wealth would not induce me to manufacture evidence making it appear that an innocent man was a criminal."

There came a pleased look to the old lady's face and she said:

"I said that to try you. I know now I can trust you — yes, trust your honor and your judgment. I will amend my answer. It will please me very much to learn that the young man is innocent. All I ask of you is to prove his guilt if he is guilty, his innocence if he is innocent."

"With that understanding I will undertake the case, and I will say here that at present evidences point to the suspicion that he is a guilty man, possibly guilty of the crime of murder."

The old lady dropped her voice and her utterance was husky as she asked:

"What evidence have you?"

"No evidence yet, but I have a suspicion. I propose to follow it up."

"Tell me about it."

"I can tell you nothing at present. My first object will be to establish the fact that Alphonse Donetti is in America, and that he wrote the note to you. I will communicate with you later."

The detective went straight to the Tombs. He was admitted to the cell of one of the burglars. He was under a new disguise and he played a great game for information. His object was to identify Alphonse Donetti with the burglars. He did not succeed, but by skillful maneuvering he got a hint that caused him to pay a visit to an outlying district on Long Island, where there is located quite a colony of Italians. It was a warm and pleasant afternoon; our hero was gotten up as Dudie Dunne, and he attracted considerable attention as a genuine chappie. Indeed, on the car when riding to his destination he was made the subject of considerable merriment by a number of men in the car. He paid no attention, but he marked one of the men pretty well. This latter individual was particularly insulting, and there was no occasion for his insults. Simply because our hero had done nothing and had a perfect right to dress as a chappie if he so elected, that fact did not warrant actual insult. As the car stopped and our hero alighted the man who had made himself conspicuous as an insulter said:

"Let's get off, fellers, and I'll give you an exhibition."

The men were under the influence of liquor and the whisky had made "Smart Alecs" of them, as it frequently does with men who have little brain and reason even when sober. The men all appeared to think it would be a good joke to see the exhibition and they left the car. Oscar had heard the man's invitation, and having made up his mind that it was an opportunity to teach one ruffian to mind his own business he took a course favorable for the exhibition, and started to go across an open lot; the men followed, and just as our hero arrived near a quagmire the man who was to give the exhibition ran forward and grasped Oscar.

The latter appeared to be terribly scared and exclaimed:

"Don't; let me alone; I have not harmed you."

"I think I know you."

"Oh, no, you don't know me — hee, hee, hee! I am a stranger around here. You are mistaken; you never saw me before."

"Yes, I have seen you before."

"You have?"

"Yes."

"Where?"

"Around here."

"Oh, no, you *are*, you *are* mistaken."

"Yes, I recognize you, mister. I saw you insult a lady — yes, I saw you insult a lady."

"Oh, no, never, never! What! I insult a lady! No, no, I admire the ladies."

"But I saw you insult one, and I am going to punish you."

"You are mistaken, my friend — yes, you are mistaken, if you saw me speak to a lady. It was a bit of gallantry, that is all. Yes, I am very gallant to the ladies, I am a sort of defender of the ladies — their champion — yes, sir, their champion."

Dudie Dunne rather spunked up in manner as he spoke, and the men all laughed merrily.

"You did insult a lady, and I challenge you to fight me."

"Ou! ou! my dear friend, you are mad!"

"Yes, I am mad enough to knock you into the middle of next week, but I am going to give you a chance. You must fight me."

"Fight you, my friend?"

"Yes, fight me."

"You had better be careful. Don't challenge me to fight you. I am a gentleman, I am, and an athlete. You are only a common man; you can't fight me."

The men all laughed at the idea of the dude's being an athlete.

"I know you are an athlete, but you must fight me all the same."

"I beg your pardon, my friend, I cannot fight you here on the public street."

"You need not fight me here."

"But I don't wish to fight you at all."

"But you must fight me."

"Where can I fight you?"

"Oh, we can go right over there in the grove — no one will see us — but you must fight."

"You do not want me to thrash you, do you?"

"Yes, I do."

"You are not seeking for a fight, are you?"

"Yes, I am."

"Why, my friend, you'll get a surprise if you fight me. I am a regular fighter, I am — hee, hee, hee! I don't want to take advantage of you."

Little did those fellows dream as they laughed that the supposed chappie was telling the truth. Indeed he had a surprise for them and he intended to work up to the climax for all it was worth.

"Come on, I am going to make you fight me."

The challenger was quite a lusty fellow, and on appearances one would have thought he would knock the chappie over with a mere side-swing of his arm.

"Say, you fellows are foolish. Don't provoke me; I am a terror — yes, I am — hee, hee, hee!"

"All right, I am looking for a terror."

"And you want me to go over to the grove?"

"Yes."

"And you insist upon it?"

"Yes, I do."

"Well, I'll go over with you."

The party, full of glee, walked over to the grove.

There was the challenger and two friends and our hero, and he amused his friends by a display of his agility, his muscle and sinew. When they reached the grove the fellow who was to fight threw off his coat and Oscar said:

"See here! It's a good deal of trouble for me to thrash you; it's like work — I don't like work. I'll give you fellows fifteen cents to go to get your beer and call it off."

The men guffawed.

"Come on," said the challenger, walking up and squaring for Oscar. The latter stood with his hands at his sides, a picture of effeminacy, but when the man tapped him on the nose a most singular and astonishing result followed. Seemingly without an exertion the dude let drive, caught his assailant and insulter on the forehead and sent him tumbling, heels up. It was one of the cleanest knock-downs on record.

CHAPTER VII

OSCAR HAD PROMISED A SURPRISE AND HE
MAKES GOOD HIS PROMISE, AND AFTER SERVING
OUT THE MAN AND HIS FRIENDS HE STARTS OUT
AND ENCOUNTERS MORE SERIOUS ADVENTURES.

Our hero had promised the men a surprise, and he kept his word. A more surprised man than the fellow who caught the stinging blow never went whirling to the ground. It is stated that a similar scene frequently occurred with Billy Edwards, the light-weight champion, years ago, who gave no evidence in his appearance of being the athlete and powerful hitter that he really was.

The man who got it was a little dazed when he recovered his feet. He looked surprised indeed, but made a rush, possibly thinking there had been some mistake and he had been kicked by a mule instead of receiving the sockdologer from the effeminate-looking dude. He made a rush, as stated, when Dudie Dunne got into shape, worked his attitude, and dancing around his antagonist a moment he let drive again, and a second time the astonished insulter and challenger went whirling to the ground, blood spurting from his nose while his eyes began to swell.

The two other men were so surprised they just stood and looked on. Indeed it was a curious sight, but Oscar did not intend them to have the laugh so easy. Like the Irishman and the bull they had had their laugh before they went over the fence. It was their turn, thought Dudie Dunne, and as he gave his first assailant the second clip he swung round and quick as a flash light of a photographer he let the two men successively have it square on the forehead and over they went, heels up. When they recovered their feet they used them — used them to good advantage — in getting away, while chappie went for number one again, but the fellow begged — - actually begged — and our hero picking up his coat flung it at him and commanded:

"Get away, you dirty dog, and mind what you are at next time you attempt to insult a man who did no harm to you."

The whole tone and manner of the supposed dude had changed, and as the three men joined each other at some distance one of them said:

"What was it we struck?"

"I reckon we struck against a stone wall or a flying brick, from the way my face is swelling."

The men had gotten their surprise, and our hero, as a matter of prudence, being alone in the grove, changed his disguise, dropped the chappie role altogether, and walked off in an opposite direction. He had visited the neighborhood for a special purpose, and his run-in with the three rowdies had only been a side diversion.

Oscar walked over to a row of dilapidated-looking houses, where he had presented a view of the miserable condition in which human beings can live and thrive. On the way over he passed the three men whom he had served out, and so complete was his disguise they failed to recognize him. He walked past the cottages several times and only attracted a passing glance; or it is more probable that those who saw him did not recognize that he had passed and repassed. Oscar was going by for the third time when he saw a face — a dark face with glittering black eyes — appear at one of the upper windows just for an instant. Our hero, however, was one of those who can take in a great deal at a glance and he muttered:

"Aha! a fish has seen the bait, now there will come a nibble."

The detective after a little passed down by the row of houses for the fourth time, and he kept his eyes seemingly in one direction, when in fact his glance was directed toward the window where for one instant he had seen the dark face. The face did not appear again, and he muttered:

"That was a nibble, sure. Now we will see."

He repassed the houses for the fifth time, going very slowly, but seemingly attracted no attention. He was aware, however, that he was being very closely observed, not from the window where he had seen the face, but by a female and a rather pretty-looking young Italian woman, and as our hero passed she smiled upon him very sweetly — and she could smile sweetly — and her glittering black eyes were illuminated with a brilliance that was charming.

Our hero stopped short, stepped toward the stoop on which the girl was sitting, and asked:

"Do you speak English?"

"Yes," came the answer, and again the maiden smiled a bewildering smile.

"Do you live in these houses?"

"Yes."

"Do you know a young lady named Fennetti?"

"That is my name," and the girl smiled even more sweetly than before. The detective did not smile, however, but the regret shot through his mind: "Why in thunder did I chance to pitch upon that name?"

"I am looking for a Miss Fennetti, a drawing teacher."

"I am a drawing teacher," came the startling answer.

The detective for a moment was knocked endways, but he was a young officer of wonderful resource and he said:

"I am glad to meet you. I was told that you could tell me where I can find a gentleman named Argetti."

Our hero had manufactured the name, but the dark-eyed beauty with the glittering black eyes at once answered:

"I know Signor Argetti."

The detective was matched, but he discerned that he had not only caught a nibble, but a regular bite, and he was in danger of being bitten if he did not play just right.

He was the cool-headed, nervy man to do it, however, and he said:

"Will you furnish me the direction?"

"I will take you to his house."

"Oh, do you know where he lives?"

"Yes."

"Is it far from here?"

"Yes."

The girl had made a slip. She had given our hero a chance to hedge. She was bright and smart, but she would have been a mind-reader had she successfully parried our detective clear to the end of his diplomacy. He appeared to stop and think, and the girl asked:

"Shall I guide you?"

"I was thinking."

She exclaimed quickly:

"It is not very far. It will only take us about ten minutes."

While talking to the pretty Italian girl our hero was letting his glance wander around. He was looking for a *bigger fish*. The girl, meantime, raised her hand to her brow as though to recall something to her mind; as she did so Oscar observed a gem of rare value glittering on her finger, and mentally he ejaculated:

"Aha! I reckon I am getting into deep water."

"Will you go?" she asked.

"And you will guide me?"

"I will."

"My business with Mr. Argetti is not really pressing, but I will go for the pleasure of having such a lovely guide."

"Hold! hold! no flattery, please. I am merely obliging a stranger."

The girl's eyes flashed with a different light than that which illuminated them when her eyes embellished her smile.

"I don't mean to flatter you. I but spoke the truth."

"You wish to see Signor Argetti personally?"

"Yes."

"You will not be able to see him before night."

"And will I be compelled to wait until to-night?"

"To see him, yes."

"Can you not go and show me where his house is located, and then I can call upon him at my leisure?"

"I cannot go with you until to-night."

Again the girl smiled one of her bewildering smiles.

"At what hour shall I come here?"

"At about nine o'clock."

"And then I will surely find him at home?"

"Yes."

"And you will meet me to guide me to his home?"

"Yes."

"Where?"

"At the railroad crossing."

"You will be there at nine?"

"I will."

"I will meet you and be very much obliged to you," said our hero, and raising his hat like an Italian count he walked away.

Oscar understood his risk, but he understood more. He knew that he was on the track of some one. A great game had been played. He connected all the little incidents — the face at the window, the dark face of a man with glittering eyes, then the woman so handily on the stoop of an adjoining house. Then again her admissions to a false identity, for our hero had invented both names that he had given the girl. All these little incidents proved that he had been observed, that he had aroused a suspicion as to his design, and that the observation and suspicion could only be aroused in one who feared something — possibly feared being seen and tracked.

After the girl had seen our hero pass from view, she entered the house at the window of which Oscar had seen the dark face. In the room was a desperate-looking man — a man one would fear to meet at night alone, for every lineament betrayed the man to be a desperate scoundrel.

When the girl returned the man asked, as she entered the room, he speaking in Italian:

"Who is he?"

"I do not know."

"What is his purpose?"

"I leave you to judge. I will repeat the conversation."

"Do so."

The girl exhibited a wonderful preciseness of

memory by repeating every word that had passed between herself and the stranger. The man listened, and when the recital was concluded he said:

"You are bright; you intended to be very cute, but alas! if he is a foe, as I believe he is, he invented those names. He knows you confessed to an identity that is false, and therefore knows that there is something wrong."

"What will you do?"

"He is to meet you to-night?"

"Yes."

"You are to guide him to the house of Argetti."

"Yes."

"I will be Argetti and you shall introduce him to me. He will be led to the little cabin out on the marsh. I have had it fitted up for an emergency. After you have brought him to me you must be on the watch to learn if there are others at his back; if there is you must signal me, if not you must signal me."

"And then?"

The man laughed in a strange, weird manner and said:

"I have a grave under the cabin floor."

The girl's face assumed a very thoughtful expression.

"Well, what now?"

"You may be too rash."

"How?"

"I do not think there is any necessity for putting a body in the grave. You can play a shrewder game."

"I can?"

"Yes."

"How?"

"Maintain the character of Argetti."

"That depends."

"Upon what?"

"The discoveries I make concerning this man?"

"He appears very harmless, very much of a gentleman. He may not intend harm. He may not be a foe."

"I would be glad to agree with you, but I have experience. If he were an American, I would believe as you do, but he is English."

"How do you know he is English?"

"By his dress and walk. I observed him very closely."

"Suppose he is English?"

"Then he has come over here to look for me."

"That man is not a detective."

"He is not?"

"No."

"How do you know?"

"He is a weak and very dainty young gentleman."

"Is he?"

"Yes."

"Well, I tell you that when one becomes a fugitive he must judge people by their acts, not by their looks; I believe the man is either a detective, or a detective's decoy. His innocent looks aid his trick, but I will know after he has visited me in the cabin."

"Oh, I hope you will do him no harm."

"What! has his handsome face bewitched you?"

"No."

"It would appear so."

"I would save you."

"Save me?"

"Yes."

"By having me captured. No, no, girl, I know how to take care of myself. I've been fighting the police of different countries for too many years to fear an encounter now."

At the hour named our hero was on hand, but during the time he had been waiting he had become conscious that he was under surveillance, and the man who appeared to "dog" him was an Italian. The fellow was very cute in practicing his game of dodge and peep, and our hero was unable to see his face, so he finally determined to make it a counter dodge and peep, but his man dodged out of the way like the man at the window, and Oscar lost sight of him.

As stated, he appeared at the meeting place and the girl was there waiting for him.

"You are on time," he said.

"Yes, I am here."

"You are very kind."

"I promised."

"I will pay you for the trouble you have taken."

The girl was thoughtful and silent. She did not start, but stood, as intimated, lost in deep thought. Finally she asked:

"Will you tell me why you wish to meet Argetti?"

"I wish to ask him some questions."

"No, that is not your purpose."

"Well, no, that is not my purpose, but I am permitted to name my business to Argetti only."

The girl looked around in a furtive manner and said:

"Can I advise you?"

"Yes."

"Do not go to meet Argetti to-night."

"Why not?"

"Do not ask any questions, but heed my warning."

"Is it a warning?"

"Yes."

"Why do you warn me? Why should I be warned?"

"Argetti is a peculiar man — a very suspicious man."

"Well?"

"He is a man of very violent temper. His house is situated in a very lonely place. Should he become angry he could assault you and your cries would not be heard."

"Why should he assault me?"

"I cannot imagine, and yet I am warned that it is not best for you to go there to-night."

"Yes, I must go."

"Your business must be very urgent."

"It is."

"I have warned you."

"Yes, but you should give me more definite information."

"I cannot."

"What would you have me do?"

"Don't go, and I will tell him you failed to meet me."

"Aha! he is waiting for me. Then he knows of my intended visit?"

"Yes, that is why I did not guide you to his house this afternoon. I desired to prepare him for your visit."

The girl discovered her error by the admission that our hero was expected, but she was quick in seeking to repair her error and besides she was taking chances at best.

"I shall go and meet him."

"You are a gentleman."

"I trust so."

"I have warned you."

"You have."

"You will not betray me?"

"Not for my life."

"I believe you, and trust all will come out well, but I tell you plainly you are taking great chances as I am."

"You are?"

"Yes."

"How?"

"In warning you. If it were known that I had warned you it would cost me my life."

"You are very frank."

"I am."

"Why?"

"Because I fear you will be made the victim of another man."

"The victim of another man?"

"Yes."

"Explain."

"I told you Argetti had a foe."

"Yes."

"He knows that foe is seeking him."

"Yes."

"He has heard of your inquiring for him."

"Yes."

"He associates you with his enemy; if it were his enemy I would utter no words of warning, but believing you are my friend I warn you."

The detective put two and two together and at once concluded that the man who had been watching him during the afternoon was the foe of the so-called Argetti. This man had been watching our hero because he believed he was in communication with Argetti, or the individual whom the so-called Argetti represented.

The detective meditated and finally said:

"I must see Argetti."

"You fully comprehend what I have said?"

"I do."

"You know there is risk?"

"I do."

"You know that I have advised you in all sincerity?"

"Yes."

"Do you really go alone to meet Argetti?"

"I do."

"Very well, we will go."

CHAPTER VIII

OUR HERO GOES TO THE LONE HOUSE ON THE MARSH — HE MEETS THE DESPERATE-LOOKING MAN AND SOME VERY FINE DIPLOMACY FOLLOWS, ALSO STRANGE AND WEIRD SUGGESTIONS.

The girl did not speak another word following her remark, or rather command, as recorded at the close of our preceding chapter; and soon she turned aside to take the path through the marsh, and for the first time spoke. She said:

"That is the house where you see the glimmer of a light."

"I thought that light was on some vessel in the bay."

"No, it is a cabin, and there is not another dwelling within a mile and a half at least."

"You have been very kind to warn me."

"Yes."

"Is the man's name Argetti whom we are to meet?"

"He will answer for Signor Argetti."

"He is a gentleman, I suppose."

At that moment the girl stopped short. She faced our hero and said:

"You have not kept faith with me."

"I have not?"

"No."

"How have I failed?"

"You have brought others with you. I tell you frankly I will warn Argetti."

"On my honor, I have not brought any one with me."

"We have been followed."

"Then our follower is the real foe of Argetti."

"Do you know him?"

"I do not."

"I shall warn Argetti."

"Do so."

"And you are willing that I should warn him?"

"Yes."

"I will tell him my suspicion."

"Very well, do so; there is no deceit in my visit to Signor Argetti."

The girl hesitated a moment and then said:

"Very well, I am but obeying orders all round. We will proceed."

Our hero was very handsomely attired, and he looked like a very effeminate young man — one who possessed neither courage nor stamina. Indeed, from his appearance, a resolute, sturdy man might expect to deal with him as he would with a mere boy. But our hero was one of those who expanded in a crisis.

The girl upon reaching the cabin rapped on the door and from the inside came the demand:

"Who's there?"

"I am here."

"Alone?"

"No, the gentleman is with me."

"Come in."

The girl pushed the cabin door open, and our hero entering found himself in a dimly-lighted apartment and in the presence of a villainous, dark-faced man. The latter eyed his visitor by the aid of the dim, flickering light shed abroad in the room by a sputtering candle.

"Be seated," said the man, and he spoke in fairly good English.

Our hero obeyed and expected the girl would tell the man that his visitor had not visited him unaccompanied, but she said nothing beyond asking:

"Shall I go?"

"Yes, you can go."

A moment later and Argetti, as the man chose to be called, and our hero were sitting face to face under the dim light of the sputtering candle. Argetti fixed his glittering eyes on our hero as though he would read him through and through, and at length, in a quick, sharp tone he said:

"You desire to see me?"

"Yes."

"Well, what is your purpose?"

"That's all," answered our hero coolly.

"That's all?"

"Yes."

"What do you mean?"

"What I say."

"But you desired to see me?"

"Yes."

"And I repeat why did you desire to see me?"

"I wanted to see what you looked like."

"And you have no special business with me?"

"No."

"Then why did you come here?"

"I wanted to see you, that's all."

"On what business?"

"No business. I merely desired to gratify my curiosity."

"Are you a fool or do you take me to be a fool?"

"Neither."

"Your conduct is so strange I do not know what to think."

"Can I trust you?"

"Yes."

"I am using you as a guy. I am seeking to fool a man."

Argetti stared with an amazed look upon his face, and our hero continued:

"Yes, I am using you as a decoy. I find I *am* being 'dogged,' by a certain man. He is on my track to-night. He was on my track this afternoon and I wished to act very mysterious and fool him, so when the girl asked my business this afternoon I told her I was looking for a gentleman named Argetti. My answer was a 'steer,' but the girl said she knew Argetti. I had invented the name and was surprised, so I conceived a desire to see the individual. I had, as it appears, individualized, for I knew no Argetti until the girl said she knew the man. Is your name Argetti?"

"Permit me, please, to think over what you have said, and to ask you a few questions."

"Good. I will answer your questions like a little man."

Argetti appeared more and more amazed, and he sat for a long time eyeing our hero without speaking one word. The interview would appear to have been very embarrassing. When Argetti spoke there was a depth of suppressed passion in his tone.

"Have you come here to amuse yourself at my expense?"

"Yes," came the bold and really insulting answer.

The Italian leaped to his feet exclaiming:

"You miserable little fool, I'll wring your neck as I'd wring the neck of a squab."

Oscar did not move or betray any fear or nervousness. He merely laughed his "hee, hee, hee!" and said soothingly:

"Now don't become violent, old fellow; don't become violent, even if I am having a little fun at your expense."

"You dare tell me you are here to have fun at my expense?"

"Certainly," came the brazen answer.

The very boldness and indifference of the detective appeared so paralyze to the Italian.

"Do you know the risk you take?"

"Certainly."

"You think I am a mere puppet for your amusement?"

"Certainly, but don't get violent, for I am an awful fellow when I get roused. Sometimes I have a spell come over me — yes, a strange sort of spell — and then I become very, very violent. So don't arouse me and bring on one of those spells. Just sit down and let me amuse myself at your expense. This is a very novel amusement for me. The idea of facing a terrible man right in his den and enraging him. Why, it's just jolly."

The Italian's eyes glowed like coals of fire as he said:

"You are lying; you came here with a purpose; you came back with friends whom you think you can summon at a moment's notice; but they will never come; I have taken care of them, and you are at my mercy. I have a grave all prepared under this flooring, and unless you give a satisfactory explanation of your visit here *you* will occupy that grave."

"Well, well, you are very amusing. You act just like some terrible brigand. I guess you were a brigand in your own country."

The words had just escaped our hero's lips when

with a yell the Italian leaped upon him. Oscar was prepared for the spring. He leaped to his feet in time to meet his assailant, and in true fistic style, as the man attempted to seize hold of him, our hero let fly and caught his dark-faced assailant on the chin and over the man went. But with a yell he leaped to his feet, drew a poniard and made a rush; but here our hero, cool as an icicle, was prepared for the would-be murderer. He had drawn a club, dealt the Italian a blow on the hand which knocked the knife from his grasp, and then dealt him a powerful stroke on the head which brought him to his knees, and at the same instant the door opened and the Italian girl peeped into the room. She immediately withdrew. Our hero had the so-called Argetti laid out. The man was not only dazed by the force of the blow, but he was paralyzed with surprise. Here he, a great, powerful bull-necked man, had been knocked down with perfect ease apparently by an effeminate dude, and when he had drawn his knife he was disarmed and brought to his knees with blows from a club in the hands of the same dude in appearance. The Italian recovered from his surprise and curses fell from his foaming lips. He looked like a raging demon, so great was his anger — he leaped to his feet and sought to seize hold of a stool, but ere he could do so he received a second rap on the head which knocked him face foremost to the floor; then Oscar sprang forward, rolled the man over and clapped a pair of darbies on his wrists, and having his man thus helpless he coolly returned, took his seat and waited for the man to arise and speak. The man rolled over and lay on his back and glared at his conqueror.

"Well, Argetti," said Oscar with his "hee, hee, hee! — you have come to grief. Well, you are a very violent man. I warned you — hee, hee — yes, I told you I was bad when aroused; that I was subject to strange spells. You believe me now, and please just lie still and let me amuse myself. You have given me more amusement than I expected. I like to knock men down and bring them around — it's real fun."

"You will pay for this fun."

"Yes, certainly, I intend to give you half a dollar, and — hee, hee, hee — that's an awful big sum of money for just a little amusement. I once gave a dollar for the privilege of beating a man almost to death, but I nearly killed him, you know, and I've only hammered you just a little — yes, just a little — I did give you one hard rap, though — yes, one hard rap — hee, hee, hee!"

The agonies expressed in the face of Argetti are indescribable. He glared and writhed, and his face worked as though in a convulsion, but when he managed to calm himself sufficiently to again speak he said:

"Now, I am at your mercy, why am I arrested?"

"Arrested?"

"Yes."

"Who said anything about arrest?"

The man held up his manacled hands.

"Ah, that is a part of my amusement; but here, let's see if you know anything? Are you acquainted with Alphonse Donetti?"

A look of abject terror succeeded the former expression of rage and disappointment that had distorted Argetti's face, and when our hero saw this change to a look of terror there came a rapid beating of his own heart.

"I never heard the name. It is another name of your invention, I think."

The detective laughed and said:

"How strange it is that I so readily invent names of

real personages. Why, I really begin to suspect that your name is truly Argetti."

"Why did you ask about Alphonse Donetti?"

"Then you do know him?"

"No, but as you have mentioned that name it may aid me in explaining some grave mistake that has been made in my arrest."

"Oh, there is no such person as Donetti. I was fooling you — hee, hee, hee — but don't you know why the irons were put on you?"

"I do not."

"You have a short memory."

"My memory don't aid me in that direction."

"It don't?"

"No."

"Then you must forget that without provocation you set to murder me, and you have the cheek to ask why you are arrested, and intimate there has been a mistake. No, no, there has been no mistake. You were arrested for an assault upon me — an attempt to murder me."

"But you are an intruder in my house — you may be a robber."

"I beg your pardon, I was introduced into your house, and you rather inveigled me here. I didn't know before, but now I begin to suspect that you are a very bad man. It is possible that you have committed a very serious crime in Italy, or you wouldn't be so infernally sensitive — hee, hee, hee!"

When our hero made an allusion to a possible crime in Italy the man actually groaned, but said nothing.

Our hero had his prisoner, and the question arose, What should he do with him? He had started out alone; he had no one to aid him. For some time he meditated. It was necessary to have some charge upon which to arrest

the man, and he determined to carry out a bold proceeding. He tied and bound his man, so he could not
move. Indeed, without assistance it would have been
impossible for him to get free, and during the process,
Argetti, as we will call him, said:

"You will regret what you are doing. I am a person of
some quality, and you will be held to a bitter responsi-
bility."

"Very well, I like to hold responsibilities, that will just
suit me — hee, hee, hee!"

Having secured and gagged his man our hero slipped
forth from the cottage. He looked around for the Italian
girl. He did not see her, and he muttered:

"Hang it! I am anchored here; that girl will steal in
and release the man." Even as our hero spoke he heard a
shrill scream, and it was the voice of a female and not
very far distant. He started at a run in the direction from
which the scream had come and quickly arrived at a
point where he beheld a man struggling with a woman.
Oscar dashed forward, the man saw him, released the
girl, and our hero saw her fall to the ground. He believed
a murder had been committed and he ran past the girl to
secure the murderer. The latter proved fleet of foot, and
most mysteriously disappeared. He vanished as com-
pletely as though he had been suddenly dissolved into
air.

"Well, that gets me," he ejaculated, and after standing
for some minutes looking in every direction, he returned
to where the girl lay. He expected to find her dead, but as
our hero approached she rose to her feet.

"Thank heaven!" ejaculated Oscar, "I thought you
had been murdered."

"I believe he intended to murder me and he might
just as well have succeeded — my life is forfeited now."

"Your life is forfeited?"

"Yes."

"Why do you say that?"

"Those men suspect me; you have given my life away."

"I have given your life away?"

"Yes."

"How?"

"By your assault upon Argetti. I did not suspect that were an officer. They will claim that I knew — that I was in league with you, and led Argetti into the trap."

"Is that man's name Argetti?"

"No, but that is the name you gave him. We will speak of him as Argetti."

"You know his real name?"

"I do."

"What is his real name?"

"I dare not tell you. I have already forfeited my life."

"Who is the man you were struggling with?"

"One of Argetti's confederates — one of the gang."

"You need not fear to confide in me. You have not forfeited your life. You shall be protected at all hazards."

"Ah, you do not know."

"Do not know what?"

"The desperate character of these men."

"What relation do you bear to these men?"

"I am an orphan; my parents died in an English poor-house. This man Argetti adopted me as his child. I have traveled all over the world with him, but now I must flee away and hide somewhere."

"You need not flee away. Argetti, as we call him, can do you no harm. We will take care of him."

"But his confederates. Already one of them has made an attempt to strangle me."

"Who was the man?"

"I did not recognize him. Probably Argetti had him as a reserve after he had settled you. Oh, how unfortunate I am, to be associated with these men, and yet I have never committed a crime. I have no proof concerning any particular crime they have committed, and yet I am sure they are criminals. But see there!" suddenly exclaimed the girl, pointing to a shining object lying on the ground.

CHAPTER IX

OSCAR PRESSES FORWARD AND MAKES SOME STARTLING DISCOVERIES — ALSO ENCOUNTERS A CONTINUOUS LINE OF ADVENTURES.

Dudie Dunne did not know whether to believe the girl's statements or not. He was compelled to admit a partial verification, as he certainly had seen her struggling in the hands of a man, and again there was no need for her to announce the fact that Argetti was a criminal unless she spoke the truth. He stooped down and picked up the glittering object from the ground. It proved to be a small miniature that could be worn on a watch chain. He drew his little mask lantern, flashed its light on the painted face, and uttered a cry of amazement. It was a most thrilling revelation that came to him. It was beyond all question the face of Alphonse Donetti. It had probably been torn off his guard chain during his struggle with the girl. He was a confederate of Argetti. He was a would-be assassin. Alas! he had no cheerful news for poor Alice Frewen, but he was verging toward a startling discovery, leading up to a clue to the solution of the Roman robbery and murder.

"What is it?" asked the girl.

"It's a miniature."

"Let me see it."

Oscar held the light on the picture so the girl could

see it. She looked at it intently and said:

"He is one I never saw before, but he is undoubtedly a confederate, and he believes I betrayed Argetti. It is a wonder he did not attack you."

"He merely sought to revenge his pals on you; but now what shall we do?"

"I must flee away."

"No, you will go with me. I will find a home for you."

As the detective spoke he flashed the light of his lantern square on the girl's face. Hers was indeed a remarkable face. She was very beautiful, and there was an expression upon it which Oscar, despite his discerning powers, could not interpret.

"Do you wish me to go with you?"

"Yes."

"Why?"

"You have done me a service and in so doing have run yourself into peril. I must see that no harm comes to you."

"You may intend to use me as a witness."

"It is possible."

"Then I cannot go with you. I will never turn against that man."

"Are you under any obligations to him?"

"He never abused me. He was fond of me — treated me with great kindness, although he is a very desperate man. No, you must be satisfied with what service I have done you; I can never turn witness against him. I trust to your generosity to save me this trial."

"I will promise not to call upon you as a witness."

"I had long determined to flee away. I was not satisfied with my life with that man, although I cannot complain of his treatment. He gave me plenty of money, bought me expensive clothing, gave me jewels. He claims

I am his niece; I do not believe it is a true claim."

"You say he gave you jewels?"

"Yes."

"Then he must have money."

"He is rich."

"How it is he lives in such miserable quarters?"

"That is a hiding place. He dwells there to hide his identity, but he has an elegant residence in New York. It is only within the last few weeks that he took up his abode in those miserable quarters where you found me."

"You were disposed to act as his confederate when I first met you."

"Yes, but I relented and I tried to give you warning; you would not heed me."

Our hero recalled the warning words, and she continued:

"I suddenly resolved to carry out my design and flee away. I wished to save your life, for I believed you were in peril. When you passed our house he looked from the window and concluded you were searching for him. He evidently within the last few weeks has feared pursuit. I acted under his instructions. I did not dare refuse, but I did seek to save you. Then I concluded you were perfectly able to take care of yourself. The result proves my conclusion correct."

Our hero had obtained a great deal of suggestive information, but a little discovery had caused him considerable discomfort. He had hoped to reach a different result in his investigations concerning Alphonse Donetti. He feared now that the very worst construction must be placed upon his character and career.

"Where is the house of Argetti in New York located?" he asked.

"I cannot tell you."

"You do not know?"

"I know, yes, for in that house are many articles of great value belonging to me."

"Presents from Argetti?"

"Yes."

"I am afraid it is dangerous property for you to claim."

"I shall never claim anything except the money. I will need that when I flee."

"Where will you go? Will you return to Italy?"

"No, I dare not go there."

"And your money is in that house?"

"Yes."

"Let me see. We will go to New York at once, and you shall go and get the money and then report back to me."

"No, I shall not go there to-night."

"Why not?"

The girl made no answer.

The detective again meditated; he recognized that he had a very bright and shrewd person to deal with, and he said:

"Very well, then return to your humbler home to-night, and I will call out and see you to-morrow."

"No, I will not return there."

"Why not?"

"I dare not. The attack upon me proves that I am under suspicion. Argetti's friends would not spare me."

"Do his neighbors know his character?"

"No."

"Did he have visitors at the house where I first met you?"

"No."

"Then how do you know he has those confederates?

"They called upon him frequently at his home in

New York. They must have warned him of danger."

"You can return to your late home. Argetti will not return to that house. I shall take him to New York as a prisoner."

"Then I must disappear at once."

"Will you meet me to-morrow?"

"Yes."

"Where?"

"I will meet you to-morrow night."

"In New York?"

"Yes."

"Very well, meet me at —." Our hero named a place and said he would walk back with her. She asked to be permitted to proceed alone.

"Very well, I shall remain here until morning to watch my prisoner, but to-morrow night I will meet you in New York at the place named."

"I will meet you," said the girl.

The reader will learn later on why our hero was apparently so slack in permitting the girl, under all the circumstances, to go away alone. She started off and he returned to the cabin. Once inside he determined to take great chances. He did not remain in the cabin, but returned by a straight cut across the meadows to the vicinity of the row of houses where Argetti had his home. His wisdom was justified. He saw the girl enter the house. He lay round and later saw her come forth, although it was after midnight. He had worked a transform and started on the track. She took the cars for New York; he rode with the engineer on the engine of the elevated train. She did not see him when she reached the ferry. He crossed with her and on the New York side luck favored him. He met a brother detective. He had just time to give the latter some directions, and he fell to the girl's trail again. He had made up his mind as to the course he would take, and again his conclusions were justified in the most startling manner. He had anticipated her design and in following her he had been compelled to be very careful, for he speedily discerned that she was on the watch against being followed. She evidently suspected that she would be, and Oscar had lain very close in order to avoid observation, but he was delighted at the prospect of witnessing the verification of his suspicions. The girl finally arrived in front of a very nice house — one of those narrow houses to be found uptown in New York in very stylish neighborhoods. The detective was actually compelled to throw himself at full length beside the curb in order to avoid observation, and he actually crept forward like a huge snail, for the girl was very cute and careful in ascertaining whether she was being followed or not. At length our hero's patience and endurance were rewarded; he saw the girl ascend the stoop of a house, produce a key and enter; and he then knew that she had returned to the lodging place back of Brooklyn — to Argetti's poorer quarters — for the very purpose of getting this key. She passed inside the house, and then Dunne rose to his feet, ran forward and darted down to the basement door of the house. Once under the stoop it took him but a little time to open the door, and he too passed inside the house. He did not stop to take observations, but hastened up the stairs, and in the rear room on the second floor he saw the glimmer of a light. It was a critical moment, but he was a winner. He made no hesitation in entering the room. He did not stop to watch the girl. He was fully satisfied in having located the house. He felt he could trust himself for all other discoveries. He peeped into the room and beheld the girl standing before a mirror, and for the first time only realized how singularly beautiful she was. He stepped into the room; the girl was so intent gazing at her beautiful self in the mirror she did not hear his entrance, but suddenly as she beheld his reflection in the glass she uttered a suppressed scream and turned and faced him with the startled exclamation, "You here!"

"Yes."

"This is treachery."

Oscar smiled and said:

"Do not use so harsh a term."

"It is indeed treachery; you were to meet me to-morrow night."

"Yes, and I will. I did not *meet* you this time, I followed you."

"You now have sealed my doom. They will follow me to the end of the world. They will know beyond all question that I am a traitress, or they will assume so."

"I repeat, you need not fear these men."

"I do not see how you succeeded in following me. I thought it possible and I watched; you were very clever."

"Cleverness comes in the way of business with me."

"What did you do with Argetti?"

"He will be in jail ere sunrise."

"Then ere sunrise I must be as far from New York as I can get."

"You will not get far."

"I will not get far?"

"No."

"What do you mean?" demanded the girl, her face assuming a ghastly hue.

"You are not the master of your own movements."

The look that overspread the beautiful girl's face was pitiful to behold, and she exclaimed in a tone of heart-breaking sadness:

"Then you have betrayed me."

"No, I have not betrayed you. I have simply made you my prisoner."

"I am your prisoner?"

"Yes."

Our hero spoke in a stern voice.

There came a look of agony to the girl's face as she murmured:

"It is as I feared; it is all over."

As she spoke she drew something from the bosom of her dress and was carrying it to her lips, but the detective was too quick for her. He leaped forward and seized her wrist. She sought to struggle, but in his powerful grasp her struggles soon ceased, and as she stood pale, trembling and helpless, she said:

"Please let me die."

"Why do you wish to die?"

"I do not want to live."

"Answer me one question: are you a criminal, and do you fear to live?"

"I am not a criminal. What I told you was the truth."

"Then why do you wish to die?"

"Better die now and at once rather than endure the agonies of constant suspense. Let me die, and I will but anticipate the dagger of the assassin."

"What is your name?"

"What difference does it make to you?"

"Tell me."

"My name is Caroline Metti."

"Caroline, if what you told me earlier in the night was the truth this is the most fortunate night of your life; you have more reason to desire to live now than you ever had before."

"Do not mock and taunt me."

"I am neither mocking nor taunting you. I am telling you the truth."

"I do not understand what you mean."

"You will have different surroundings the rest of your life. You have won my interest and sympathy."

"And yet you have made me your prisoner."

"Only to save you against yourself. I would not bring harm to a hair of your head. I desire to save your life and your soul."

"Why?"

"Because I believe you are an unfortunate person and that you mean well, and now as far as these men are concerned you are free from them forever, I care not how many there are of them. Argetti is doomed, and every one of his friends, including the man who assailed you, will either be captured or driven from the country. A way will be provided for you to support yourself in independence. That is what I mean, and now I have something to tell you. I will be compelled to treat you as a prisoner for a little while. I do not wish to make you a party in any way to what I propose to do."

The girl appeared perplexed when our hero put handcuffs on her wrists, and after a moment in a very disconsolate tone she said: "I am not deceived; I know I am doomed. Very well, proceed. The time will come when I will have a chance to free myself."

CHAPTER X

OSCAR MAKES A THOROUGH SEARCH OF THE
HOUSE, AND AT FIRST ONLY FINDS CERTAIN
CLUES, BUT IN THE END HE MAKES A GREAT
DISCOVERY.

Dudie Dunne, having a certain purpose to carry out, paid little heed to the girl's disconsolate remarks. He knew that she would be all right in the end. He commenced and searched that house from top to bottom, and found many little articles which he put aside for future reference. He also made notes of several matters, and finally, concluding his search, he returned to the room where he had left the girl Caroline. He found her sitting on a chair, her head cast down, and she was evidently lost in deep thought. "Come," he said, "we will go."

"We will go?"

"Yes."

"You intend to keep me a prisoner?"

"Yes, for the present, and for your own safety. Some very startling events are transpiring, and it is necessary for your own safety that you should be in a safe place."

The detective led the girl to the home of a woman who had once been a prison matron. She was a very able woman. He placed the girl Caroline in this woman's charge with full instructions how to act. He had permitted the girl to take what she desired from the house, but to his surprise she took but very little — none of the elegant clothes — -none of the gems; even the ring she wore on her finger she cast upon the bureau. Our hero did not urge her to take anything, but he did secure these gems, holding them for future identification.

On the day following the incidents we have described, Oscar visited headquarters and learned that the chief had received a telegram stating that a representative of the illustrious Roman family was already on his way to New York and would probably arrive almost any day.

"He must have started for New York immediately following the sending of the cablegram."

"Yes."

"You telegraphed no particulars."

"No, I suppose they believe we have certain clues, and instead of writing they have determined to come direct to New York."

"So much the better. I believe we will have some very startling news for this representative when he arrives."

The chief and Oscar had some further conversation, the nature of which will be explained later on.

Several days passed and our hero devoted himself to one object. He tried to trail down Alphonse Donetti. In the meantime he held an interview with Alice Frewen. He had discovered the extraordinary interest of that fair, innocent, but resolute girl in the young Frenchman, and he sought to prepare her for the terrible revelations that were to come. Oscar was thoroughly convinced that young Donetti was a villain of the worst type and the confederate of villains. He was convinced that the young man had been concerned in the Roman robbery.

One evening he called at the home of Mrs. Frewen.

The latter was out, but Alice came down to meet the officer. Her manner was like one under a great mental strain.

"What have you learned?" she asked.

"Miss Frewen," said our hero, "I wish you would let me know just the extent of your interest in this young man."

"My interest in him is kept alive because of my absolute belief in his innocence. I believe he has been wronged from his cradle. I believe that under terrible temptations he has remained honorable and true."

"But has he not to your knowledge led a rather fast life in Paris?"

"I have no proof that he has."

"Answer me one more question: Have you communicated with him since he has been in America?"

The girl started and exclaimed:

"Then you know he is in America?"

"Yes, I have the most positive proof that he is in America."

"Have you seen him?"

"Yes, I have seen him."

"Why do you not tell me all about it?"

"Because I do not know how deeply I may wound you if I tell you the whole truth."

"If the truth, as you term it, is a reflection upon his honor you need not fear to tell me, for I know that you have been misled."

"You are firm in your trust in his honor and good character?"

"I am."

"Poor girl! you are infatuated and deceived."

"You may think so."

"I have the proofs."

"Satisfactory to you, no doubt, but not proofs after all."

"I know he is associated with vile characters."

"I don't doubt it," came the answer.

"You don't doubt it?"

"No."

The detective gazed aghast as he exclaimed:

"And you still maintain his integrity?"

"I do."

"I cannot understand."

"No; some day you will understand it."

"I saw him attempt a crime. I prevented him from committing what I believe would have been a murder."

"Not a murder," replied Alice.

Oscar Dunne was no fool, but he was perplexed, for he discovered at last that the girl Alice possessed certain information that she was withholding.

"There is something you know that you have not revealed to me."

"I know that Alphonse is an honorable man and incapable of committing a crime."

"You had better reveal everything to me."

"I have revealed all there is to reveal. He is an honorable man, and in the end will establish his character before the world. He has a powerful enemy, one who should be his first friend, but the day will come when his honor will be fully vindicated, and he will stand before the world with a splendid reputation. I know it, and now all I can say to you is, hold your judgment until the denouement."

When Oscar left the presence of Alice he had subject for considerable meditation. "That girl knows something," he said. He walked along thinking over the dialogue, when suddenly his attention was attracted by a struggle. He saw several men slashing at each other with knives, as he recognized by occasional bright steel gleams under the gaslight. He always carried his club with him. He ran forward and, seeing two against one, went for the two who he observed were the assailants, while the other was acting on the defensive. Oscar drew his club, and the men were so intent upon their scheme of murder they did not mind his approach, but two raps from his club sent both to the ground, and when they regained their feet they made off, while our hero sought to learn the cause of the attack from the party who had been assailed.

The man had staggered up against a railing in front of a house and his drooping attitude revealed to our hero that he was wounded.

"You are injured," said our hero.

"Yes, the cowards came upon me from behind and plunged their knives into me."

Oscar approached closer to the man and with a start that almost caused him to utter an unguarded exclamation he recognized the wounded man as Alphonse Donetti.

"You had better let me take you to a hospital."

"No, I am much obliged. I will not go to a hospital. I can take care of myself. If I live you will have saved my life, for they intended to finish me. I thank you for your intervention. I will be able to reach my home and will send for a surgeon."

"Permit me to call a carriage, and I will accompany you to your home."

The wounded man looked closely at our hero, saw that he was a gentleman, and said:

"Yes, I need some one to close my eyes. You appear to be a kind man; if it is not too much trouble secure a carriage."

Oscar did not have to go far before he found a carriage, and when he returned he found the young man still alive and apparently, under all the circumstances, singularly strong.

He assisted him into the carriage and asked:

"Where shall we drive?"

"I don't know. I'll not go to my hotel in this condition; it will occasion too much talk."

"Will you let me take you to a lodging where your condition will not attract attention?"

"Yes; I will see that you are well remunerated."

Oscar and several of the detectives had a house, an emergency house they called it. It was the very house to which he had taken Caroline Metti. He told the driver where to go and in a few moments the carriage came to a halt. Our hero discharged the coach and assisted his companion into the house, led him up the stairs to a room on the second floor, and Mrs. Keller, the woman, appeared to ask if she could be of any service.

"I will summon you if I need you," was the answer.

In the carriage the wounded man had said:

"Do not send for a physician until I learn the full extent of my wound."

Once in the room the young man looked at our hero and at once exclaimed:

"What! you?"

"Aha! you have seen me before!"

"I have."

"When and where?"

"We will not discuss it now. We will look at my wound."

The young man tore off his clothing, and going to a mirror began to look himself over. He was as cool as though merely looking for a wart. Oscar also was cool and aided in the examination.

The young man Alphonse Donetti, after a moment, said:

"I am fortunate."

"You are?"

"See, it is not a bad wound; the rascal meant to drive the knife through my heart from behind. He has merely driven his blade deep into my shoulder. I can take care of this wound myself. I do not need a surgeon."

The young man gave directions — indeed he appeared to know as well what to do as a surgeon; and one fact impressed itself upon our hero's mind: the fact that the wounded man was prepared to take great chances for his life without the aid of a physician, and this circumstance in itself was very suspicious, and, coupled with facts known to our hero, only confirmed the worst suspicious that had arisen in his mind. He followed directions, however, and the wound in a little time was properly attended to, and then seating himself in a chair Alphonse asked with perfect coolness:

"Is it convenient to you for me to remain in this room for a few days?"

"Yes."

"I will tell you frankly," said Alphonse, "I wish to avoid observation; in fact, I wish to conceal myself for a little time, especially until I recover, and if it is convenient for me to remain here this is very fortunate for me."

Oscar studied the young man's face and was forced to admit that he saw no signs of the villain. Indeed it was a singularly refined face, a classic face, more, a princely face.

"You may think it all very strange," said Alphonse.

"Yes, it is to me."

"It is strange to me that *you*, of all men, should have been the one to save my life. I owe my life to you. Loss of blood was telling on my strength, and those assassins would have finished me if you had not come to my rescue."

"You are right, but you will prosecute those men. You know them evidently."

"No, I do not. I only know they are connected with a gang and they evidently have spotted me, as you *detectives say*."

Oscar stared in amazement.

"As we detectives say?"

"Yes."

"How do you know I am a detective?"

"I know you are a detective, and I have a still more startling announcement to make. You have saved my life, but I have been lying about expecting at any moment to go to your aid and save yours."

"Save mine?"

"Yes."

"Well, you do amaze me."

"I knew I would, and I will amaze you still more. We are engaged in the same business. We are hunting down the same gang, and I believe we have succeeded."

It is impossible to describe the sensations that ran through our hero's mind as he said:

"You amaze me."

"I will be perfectly frank with you. I know all about you."

"Why did you not seek me?"

"I had made up my mind to do so. I was waiting for you to come from the house you had entered when I was assailed by those two men; and now I will tell you my story, and I trust you will believe every word I say, for I shall tell you nothing but the truth."

"Proceed and tell me your story. I am ready to believe what you tell me, and how is it you know about me?"

"I found out who you were. I saw you first when you were on the track of that Spitzanni."

"Spitzanni?" repeated our hero.

"Yes, the man whom you tracked to the meadows, or rather you were inveigled to meet him. I was at hand to aid if it became necessary, for I also was on that man's track. I will tell you about myself." Alphonse told a story that agreed with all the detective knew of Alphonse, and proceeding said:

"A great robbery occurred in Rome. A large reward was offered for the capture of the robbers and the recovery of particular pieces of jewelry — old family heirlooms. An Italian detective in Paris engaged me to come to the United States; he believed that the robbers had fled to America. He knew I spoke both Italian and English as well as French. He speaks only French and Italian. I came here and I have been on the track of those fellows for months."

"Have you made any discoveries?"

"No discoveries connecting them with the Roman robbery, but I have established the fact that they are desperate characters. This fellow Spitzanni arrived in America just after the Roman robbery. I propose to ally myself with you, if you will permit me, and I know I can be of great service to you."

"You are acquainted with Mrs. Frewen?"

"I am. She was my mother's kindest friend, but she is bitterly prejudiced against me."

"You sent her a letter."

"I did, warning her that a robbery was contemplated. I had no positive knowledge and dared not make a direct statement, but I sent a note calculated to put her on her guard, and wished she would take the necessary precautions. I learned that she did. She called you to her aid and captured the robbers."

"That is all true, and this has been a most remarkable revelation to me, for do you know I was tracking you."

"Believing me to be connected with the gang?"

"Yes."

"Had you any grounds for suspecting me?"

"Only the fact that you were an Italian and appeared to know in advance the intentions of a gang of robbers."

"I obtained my information while trailing an Italian who is an associate of those fellows. I got into his good favor and won his confidence. I rewarded him by a warning at the last moment, and that is the way I obtained my knowledge."

"Do you know the basis of Mrs. Frewen's prejudice against you?"

"I do not. She was once my friend. She has since appeared to be my enemy."

"You were not engaged in any criminal acts?"

"Why do you ask?"

"Because Mrs. Frewen really believes you are a criminal."

"She has no basis for her belief. I never did a dishonorable deed in my life. My only crime is being a poor young man."

"Have you any suspicion as to your real parentage?"

"Aha! you have heard about me from Mrs. Frewen."

"I have."

"I have no proofs as concerns the identity of my father. I have many well-grounded reasons for believing I can identify him. I probably will never obtain the proofs, never establish my claim to a noble name."

Oscar held a prolonged conversation with Alphonse Donetti. He was perfectly frank and told him of Alice Frewen's belief in his integrity, and indeed concealed nothing. Our hero was fully convinced of the young man's truthfulness, and from him obtained many facts concerning the gang with whom Argetti was associated.

Later on the two young men parted, Alphonse promising to remain where he was until he received further information from our hero. In a later interview with the chief it was agreed to arrest every one of the Italians supposed to be connected with the gang, and on the following day a number of officers — silent and effective men — went abroad and five men were arrested, who, together with Argetti made six; and our hero had reason to believe that every man was identified with the Roman robbery.

A week passed and one day the chief sent word for Oscar to come to headquarters. Our hero meantime had been in constant communication with Alphonse, the girl Caroline Metti, and also Alice, and a perfectly free interchange of confidences had been made.

As intimated, the chief sent for Oscar, and when the latter arrived he was informed that the representative of the Roman nobleman was in New York, and awaited an interview with our hero at his hotel. Oscar proceeded at once to the hotel, bearing a card from the chief, and met a very pleasant-looking gentleman who spoke English fluently, and we will here state that more English comparatively is spoken in Italy than in France.

"I am very happy to meet you," said the gentleman, after the usual interchange of courtesies, "as I understand you have had special charge of the business of running down the robbers."

"Yes, sir."

"You have certain men under arrest?"

"I have."

"Have you any proofs against them?"

"That remains for you to determine."

"For me to determine?"

"Yes."

"How so?"

"I have in my possession certain articles; if you can identify them as part of the proceeds of the robbery in Rome we have the right men."

"Will you let me see the articles?"

"If you will accompany me I will show them to you."

We will here state that the police had taken possession of Argetti's house. They had stationed a guard over it. Oscar had visited the house many times with Caroline Metti, and after many searches had unearthed a buried casket in the cellar, and in the casket he had found a rich collection of jewels. Indeed, the robbery had been of even greater magnitude than had been reported, and among the articles stolen were jewels that had belonged to the family of the nobleman during the pontificate of Gregory XI. These were articles that had come down in the family for over five centuries and were of great intrinsic as well as historical value.

This casket had been left at the house pending the arrival of the representative from Rome, subject to positive identification.

When the casket was produced and shown to the Italian he uttered a cry of delight and amazement. Indeed he fairly danced around so great was his joy.

"Are we right?" asked Oscar.

"Right, my dear sir, you are the most wonderful man on earth. I always believed Americans were a great people, and you are the greatest American I ever met."

Our hero laughed and said:

"It was a simple matter — a very simple matter."

"Ah, to you, but to me it is a marvelous feat."

"These are the stolen goods?"

"Yes, sir."

"Are the rare souvenirs there?"

The Italian made a careful examination and finally said:

"Yes, everything is here. Of course there are some few articles missing of modern manufacture, but what my master values at millions is here. Oh, how proud, how happy he will be when he learns that I have recovered his treasures, and there is but one bit of news that I could cable to him would cause him greater joy."

Our hero stared.

"Then he has met with other losses?"

"Yes, sir."

"It is possible I can aid you in this other matter."

"No, no, the grave has closed over the one object that would have made my master's heart glad. He is an old man — will soon go to the grave himself — and with him ends the male line of the great and ancient house of Prince ——."

Our hero's heart stood still, and strange, wild thoughts flashed through his mind. He did not speak of certain facts at that moment, nor did he make further inquiries. He had the one business on hand. He said:

"We have the robbers. It will be necessary for you to communicate with the Italian consul-general and proceed in a regular and legal manner to secure the extradition of the criminals."

"Yes, I will proceed at once."

The occurrences of the succeeding two weeks would not interest our readers, as our hero's time and attention were devoted to the furnishing of the evidence that was needed to extradite the robbers. As good luck would have it, at the last moment, as is often the case, one of the men "squeaked," as the vulgar professional saying has it; that is, made a full confession implicating every one of his late pals. Then the road was clear and our hero met the representative by appointment to receive his reward and payment for services. Oscar was not unmindful of the assistance he had received from Caroline Metti and she received a handsome sum as her share, and she did not refuse it, for under the advice of our hero she had determined upon her future course.

Having settled the matter as concerned Caroline Metti our hero said:

"There is one more party who comes in for recognition — a young man."

"Name him," said the representative. "I am prepared to liberally reward every one who aided in the recovery of these precious heirlooms."

"I will not name the party. I will show you his picture, and you can probably identify him yourself."

Our hero had secured the photograph of Alphonse Donetti. He handed it to the representative in a careless manner, saying:

"That is a picture of the young man, and to him we are under great obligations in this matter."

The instant the Italian saw and fixed his eyes on the picture he recoiled like one gazing at a ghost. His eyes fairly bulged. He turned pale, trembled like an aspen leaf, and attempted to speak, but his tongue appeared to cleave to the roof of his mouth. He was unable to speak. Oscar stood by, a look of delight and gratification expressed upon his handsome face.

The detective waited. He desired to give the Italian

time to recover his composure, and finally, when the latter was able to speak, he asked in gasping tones:

"Is the original of this picture alive?"

"He is."

"His name?"

"Alphonse Donetti."

"His parentage — do you know his parentage?"

"Why do you ask?"

"Answer my question."

"When you are calmer we will talk."

"What do you mean, sir?"

"I mean that possibly there is something to be explained."

"Is it possible you gave me this picture with a purpose?"

"Yes, I handed you that picture with a purpose."

"And what was your purpose?"

"I desired to learn if you had ever seen him before."

The Italian had fully recovered command of his nerves and he said:

"No, I never saw this picture before."

"Did you ever behold the original?"

"Never."

"Then why your excitement when you beheld the photograph?"

"Was I excited?"

"Sir, you must be perfectly frank with me."

"Will you explain just what you are getting at?"

"Not until you have explained your excitement."

"I have nothing to explain."

"Neither have I."

There followed an interval of awkward silence, broken at length by the Italian who said:

"There is design in all this."

"Yes, there is design."

"You will certainly intimate your design."

"I will intimate nothing."

"What is it you demand?"

"I demand to know the cause of your excitement."

The Italian meditated a moment and then said:

"This picture bears a striking resemblance to one whom I once knew."

"Who is the party?"

"The son of the Prince of ——."

"But you said you had never seen the original."

"I never did behold the original of that picture. The prince's son is dead. He has been dead several years. He was much older than the original of this picture."

Our hero was a quick and rapid thinker and he asked:

"Is it not possible that the original of that picture is the grandson of the present Prince of ——?"

"I cannot tell; the resemblance is certainly very remarkable."

"Tell me about the prince and his son."

"I will."

"Do so."

"The son of the Prince of —— married a French lady. The marriage was a secret one. He deserted his wife and later married an Italian lady of noble birth. The second wife died without leaving any children."

"How could he desert his French wife and marry an Italian woman?"

"He secured a divorce."

"Was he justified?"

"No."

"I am glad you are so frank."

"I have no reason for being otherwise. His French wife was very proud. The prince never knew of his son's marriage to the French lady — it was a secret marriage. After the death of his Italian wife without issue the son revealed to his father, the prince, the fact of his former marriage and the fact of the birth of an heir. The son was killed in a railroad disaster, and then the old prince, being without an heir, sought to find his grandson. He spent large sums of money and succeeded in establishing the fact that his grandson also was dead. He learned that he was a spirited young fellow and had been killed in a duel."

Our hero remembered how Mrs. Frewen had aided in nursing the young man Alphonse Donetti. He guessed the whole mystery and said:

"Young Alphonse Donetti, the original of that picture, was wounded in a duel. He recovered, however, and is alive to-day, a noble young man, one whom his grandfather may proudly welcome as his heir — one well calculated to maintain all the ancient glories of his race."

Our hero proceeded and told the story of Alphonse Donetti. The Italian listened attentively and finally said, when the relation was concluded:

"I believe that indeed this young man is the legitimate heir of the great prince, and his grandfather will be the happiest man in Italy when I again cable him and tell him his heir is found alive, well, and a credit to his race."

"You can cable him, for there is no doubt as to the real identity of the young man."

Oscar and the Italian continued their talk for a long time and then our hero departed, after having arranged for a meeting between Alphonse and the representative of his grandfather.

As Oscar proceeded to the home of Mrs. Frewen he remarked:

"How wonderful are the ways of Providence, and

what strange experiences in family histories come to our profession!"

Our hero found Mrs. Frewen at home. To her he made the startling revelation, and added that he had the most positive and indisputable proofs and evidence that Alphonse was well worthy to maintain the credit of his honorable lineage.

Later the detective saw Alice. To her he also made the revelation and assured her that her confidence in the innocence and integrity of the young man had been well sustained and verified, and then he learned that Alice had really met Alphonse and had learned from him his real purpose in visiting America.

Having carried the good news to Alice, our hero proceeded to meet Alphonse. The young prince had recovered from his wound to such a degree that he was able to go out, and our hero said:

"Alphonse Donetti, I have great news for you."

The young Italian stared and our hero proceeded:

"In the most remarkable manner the mystery of your parentage has been solved."

Alphonse did not start or betray any undue emotion or excitement, and Oscar related all that had occurred, and it was then that Alphonse spoke and said:

"The question of my parentage was never a mystery to me, but I believe I inherit the pride of my race. I resolved never to claim relationship to those who had treated my mother in such a cruel manner and who appeared to hate me. I supposed they knew of my whereabouts. I should never have claimed relationship, but —" The young man stopped short for a moment and then, with a glitter in his eyes, added:

"I had all the proofs of my honorable title as the legitimate heir to the name and fortune of my cruel parent, and I did intend when they were dead in memory of my mother to establish my right to the fortune and title."

"Your grandfather is innocent in this matter. You knew that your father was dead?"

"I did not know it until you told me. I never saw my father to know him. If my grandfather seeks me I will go to him and reverence him as I trust he desires."

Later Alphonse was introduced to his grandfather's representative and easily furnished all the proofs as to his identity.

A month passed and a letter arrived from the prince. He expressed his delight, sent a large check and requested his grandson to return immediately to his ancestral home.

Alphonse did not go at once, and when he did sail for Italy there went with him his wife, the princess, who as Alice Frewen had been so faithful and true to him.

Mrs. Frewen returned with her niece to Italy. Our hero saw them off, and that same day Oscar returned and met the beautiful Caroline Metti, and in a laughing tone said:

"Now, Caroline, if I could only gather the links to prove you a princess I should be a proud and happy man."

"Those links you will never gather, but I am grateful to you, for you have restored to me an interest in life and awakened an ambition."

"And what is your ambition?"

"I hardly dare tell you."

"Yes, tell me."

"You will be jealous."

"No, I will not;" but there did come a color to our hero's handsome face.

"You are sure you will not be jealous?"

"I am sure."

"It is my ambition to become a great female detective."

"Great Scott!" ejaculated our hero, "is that all?"

"That is all. Will you aid me?"

"I will, and there is no reason why you should not become the greatest lady detective that ever lived."

"I will try."

"And I will help you."

THE END